SPYING ON THE BILLIONAIRE

RACHEL HANNA

CHAPTER 1

*D*aisy stood up on the split rail fence, her favorite pair of sneakers struggling not to slip on the old wood. She braced herself with her elbows and looked out over the vast piece of land behind her house.

They wanted to build a shopping mall. A freaking shopping mall. The ugliest of all structures, as far as she was concerned. Acres and acres of land would be ruined so that soccer moms and teenage girls could spend away their futures for crop tops and overpriced bras.

She couldn't imagine someone wanting to bulldoze the rolling hills and beautiful trees that dotted the landscape of her beloved hometown. Who needed more overpriced clothing stores and gross fast food places? She tried to imagine what the property would look like five years from now. It made her stomach ache.

She'd grown up in Thornhill, an outlying suburb of Atlanta. But with the city growing further and further outward each year, developers had set their sights on her beloved little hometown for a giant shopping mall that would attract tourists and turn Thornhill into some kind of retail Mecca.

"You're torturing yourself," her best friend, Megan, said from behind her.

"Do you remember when Ralphie Lang would bring his four-wheeler out here and ride through those mud puddles left behind after the summer rains?"

Megan giggled. "And we would purposely stand too close and get splattered with orange water?"

Daisy smiled at the memory. High school had ended almost ten years ago now, but it was still fresh in her mind. She had all of the same friends. She went to all the same places. Nothing much had changed in Thornhill, after all. And she didn't want it to. She hated change.

It wasn't like she wanted to run a farm or plant a huge garden. That had been her grandfather's domain. As much as he'd tried to teach her how to work the land they owned, she never really got the hang of it other than understanding how to drive the tractor without running it into the barn. Now, she hired a local kid to keep the grass cut on their three acres and make sure her grandmother's prized roses were in tip top shape.

But she wanted it to stay the same, all of it. Her memories were as much a part of the land as the trees that grew on it. She could still see her Papa out behind the house, the summer sunset illuminating him from behind, as he tended to his vegetable garden and cursed the rabbits that kept getting into it no matter what he did.

"You know, a mall may not be that bad. We have to drive a long way to go shopping anywhere nice."

Daisy jumped off the fence and put her hands on her hips as she glared at her friend. "You're kidding me, right?"

"Well... no...."

"Meg! You know how much this means to me! To our town! Everything will change if they build this mall. All of this land will be gone," she said, sweeping her hand behind her. "Our memories will be gone."

Megan stepped forward and touched Daisy's shoulder. "No. Our memories will always be there. But things can't stay the same forever. You know that. No one can take your memories away from you. Plus, your grandparents always wanted you to leave this tiny town and do great things."

Daisy hated change more than most people. She still lived in the house she grew up in, drove the same car she had in high school and worked at the same drug store where she got her first job. A good therapist could easily see why she was so stuck in her ways. It wasn't a mystery to those who knew her.

When her mother died, Daisy had only been nine years old. Addiction was an awful thing. Even at her young age, they'd already moved thirteen times by the time she hit fourth grade. Her father had never been part of the picture, so her grandparents had stepped in to raise her, moving her to Thornhill with them.

She'd finally gotten stability with her grandparents, and she had held onto it tightly since. Even after her grandparents had passed away, Daisy hadn't move out of their house. She didn't leave her tiny town like most of her friends had. She hunkered down, trying desperately not to lose that comforting feeling that her grandparents had brought into her life.

And now a shopping mall was coming, right outside the back fence of her property. A big, ugly, concrete monster with ugly asphalt parking lots, Black Friday sales and outsiders who would eventually come to Thornhill for "retail therapy". Yuck.

"You're not still trying to fight this, are you?" Megan asked.

"Of course I am. We have another meeting tonight." Daisy had joined a small environmental group to try to block development of the land. They were currently looking into every option, such as whether any of the hundreds of acres were Native

American burial grounds or had protected vegetation. So far, no such luck, but she was hoping Lydia Maynard, the leader of the group, would have more news at tonight's meeting.

In reality, Daisy wasn't much of an environmentalist. She just wanted her little town to stay the same. She wanted the same people, the same businesses, the same feeling she got every time she walked around the town square. It was her sanity at stake, and she was going to do whatever she had to do to keep that monstrosity from ruining her home.

"I think it's a losing battle, but I support you. You know that." Megan herself had never left Thornhill, although she talked about it almost daily. She wanted to get out, but Daisy knew some part of her didn't want to leave her best friend behind.

"Thanks... I guess," she said with a chuckle.

"You know what I think..."

"Yes, you've never been one to hold your thoughts inside of that pretty little head of yours," Daisy said as she walked past her friend, rubbing her fingers on the top of her mane of curly hair as she moved.

"It's just that I think your time would be much better spent trying to find someone... to..."

"To what? Love? Yeah, that ship has sailed. In fact, it sailed, got hit by a major typhoon and sunk to the bottom of the black, scary ocean."

"The ocean isn't black."

5

"Well, you know I'm not a big fan of the ocean, so in my mind, it's pretty black."

"I never understood that. I love the ocean. The breeze, the sand between my toes..."

"And wedged in other places it shouldn't be..." Daisy said, finishing her sentence.

Megan turned and looked at her. "I just wish you'd focus your attention on making a life for yourself, Daisy. I love you like a sister, and I want to see you break free of this little town and do all the big things we've been talking about since we were kids."

Daisy smiled. "What if I don't want to break free of this town? What if this is where I want to be?"

"You can't fool me, and you know it. You're afraid."

"Oh yeah? Of what?"

"I don't know exactly, but I know I'm right. You've got to take some chances in life. You can't just stay here and turn into one of those old maids like that woman who used to live by the old saw mill. Remember her? She had a huge wart on her nose like a cartoon character."

Daisy laughed. "I remember her! We called her Old Lady Wainwright. She had all those cats, and one of them was missing a leg. But she made great pound cake. She brought it to church picnics."

Megan rolled her eyes. "Pound cake won't keep you warm at night."

"If you eat enough of it, you'll go into a carb-induced coma, so it won't matter anyway."

Tristan Spencer wasn't a man with a lot of patience, and he was losing what little he had very quickly. As he sat in his sprawling Atlanta office, overlooking a lush park area, he rubbed his forehead harshly, trying in vain to prevent a headache from taking up residence in his skull.

"So, you're telling me that an environmental group is trying to block the development deal in Thornhill? And that this little po-dunk town with these environmental quacks could stop the mall from being built? Seriously?"

Curt, one of his many employees, sat across from him, file folder in his lap and bad news emanating from his lips.

"Look, boss, we're doing everything we can, but these people aren't quitting. We're getting a lot of bad press, and you don't want to seem uncaring about the local environment..."

Tristan slammed his hand on the hard mahogany desk. "I don't care about the local environment. That's not my job, Curt. My job as CEO of this company is to develop projects, and the mall project is top on our list right now. Whatever you and the team have to do to get this thing moved forward, do it. Schmooze local politicians. Hand candy out to kids. Have a freaking parade through town. Whatever. Just do it."

Curt stared at Tristan for a moment. "Sir, if I may say so, you seem..."

"I seem what?"

"A little more... agitated... this morning."

Tristan glared at him before sighing. "Well, if you must know, I'm a bit aggravated at the moment."

"Anything I can help with?"

"Know any nannies?"

Curt paused for a moment. "You mean like grandmas?"

Tristan rolled his eyes. "No, you moron. Nannies that take care of kids."

"Oh. Sorry. I don't have kids, so..."

"Right. Whatever. Just get out of here and get the team moving, okay?"

Curt stood and left the room without saying another word. In reality, Tristan hated being so harsh to his team, but today was just a bad day.

When he'd been working his way up the ladder of success, he had always assumed more money would lead to more happiness. Lately, he wondered if his vast amount of wealth was causing him to be more miserable than he'd be if he lived in a modest home and drove one of those compact cars he saw passing him on the freeway.

Still, being a billionaire certainly had its perks,

and one of those was good in-home childcare for his daughter, Elliana. At just eight years old, Elliana was his whole world. Her mother, who Tristan was divorced from at the time, died in a car accident when Elliana was just four years old, leaving Tristan a full-time single dad with a huge corporation to run.

He loved his daughter; adored her, actually. But it was tough to find enough time to spend with her and run his business. He tried his best, or at least that's what he told himself, but there were times that he saw fathers pushing their kids on swings at the local park and wondered what Elliana would remember about him when she was older.

Would she come to hate him? Would she even really know him?

He shook the thought from his head and looked down at the pile of papers on his desk. The work never ended. People thought billionaires had staff that did everything for them, but Tristan was a hands-on kind of person. He had employees, sure, but he micro-managed most everything, a character flaw he really didn't like about himself.

His sour mood today was the result of one person - Tatiana. Not a girlfriend, but the nanny that had been with Elliana for almost two years. She'd pulled a vanishing act on him yesterday, announcing by text that she had eloped with her boyfriend of six months and they were going to travel the world until they started their own family.

Tatiana had always been a bit of an airhead, but when she snagged a wealthy entrepreneur - who she met from working for Tristan, no doubt - she was well on her way to the life she really wanted to live. Elliana was devastated, and there was little he could do to console her. She'd already lost so many people during her young life - her mother, Tatiana, both grandmothers.

She only had her father, and he was well aware that he wasn't enough. He put his head in his hands and sighed. Finding a nanny was going to be another chore he just didn't have time for right now. Thankfully, one of his secretaries had agreed to pick Elliana up from school and bring her to his office.

"Daddy!" Elliana squealed as she ran toward his desk. He painted on his fakest smile as he scooped her up into his arms and twirled her around. Truly, she was the one bright spot in his day most of the time.

"Hey, sweet pea! How was school?"

He put her down and walked back behind his desk. "Boring. We keep going over the same stuff."

"I think that's called studying, sweetheart," he said with a smile.

"Well, I'm just glad I have two months off now!"

Tristan froze in his seat. "What do you mean, Ellie?"

"Summer break. It starts tomorrow! And I can't wait to go to the beach! Can we pick up seashells?"

She looked at him with all the enthusiasm of a kid in candy store, and Tristan felt stuck. Summer break? How could that be? He frantically pushed things aside on his desk and found the big calendar underneath. And there it was in big, bold, red marker - SUMMER BREAK.

"Oh, wow, Ellie... I totally forgot about summer break... and with Tatiana gone..."

"Daddy, you promised! We haven't gone on a vacation together since... well, I don't remember a time. We have to go, we just have to!" Her eyes were welling with tears. These weren't the pleadings of a bratty child. They were the honest requests of a little girl who needed her father to step up and spend time with her.

"Of course, El. We're going to the beach. I'm just not sure which one yet. Why don't you go to the conference room and do some coloring while I finish up my work? Then we can grab dinner at the Chinese place you love so much on the way home."

Elliana trotted off, her bright pink backpack slung over her shoulder, no doubt filled with markers and stickers, her favorite things.

"Hey, Tristan. Elliana left her lunchbox in my car." His secretary, Rita, had been with him for years. An older woman, she was always ready to lend a listening ear when he needed a motherly figure in his life.

"Listen, you know we lost Tatiana this week, right?"

"Yes. That was terrible what she did. Never did like her."

"I promised Elliana that we'd take a beach trip, so I think we're going to this little town near Savannah... January something."

"January Cove? Oh yes, I've been there a few times myself. Nice and quiet."

"Yeah, so, anyway, I need a nanny to take care of Ellie."

Rita pursed her lips and cocked her head to the side, a sure sign she didn't agree with his idea. "And why would you need a nanny if you're taking a trip to spend time with your daughter?"

Tristan sighed. "Because work never stops, and this deal in Thornhill is dicey, to say the least. Look, I wouldn't take this trip at all if Elliana hadn't put a massive guilt trip on me."

"Tristan, she needs you. She wants to spend uninterrupted time with her father. You'll never get this time back, trust me. I remember when David was a little boy and..."

He held up his hand. "Rita, before you take one of your long walks down memory lane, can you just please get me the name of a temp agency who can send a qualified nanny to meet us in January Cove?"

Rita rolled her eyes, the only one of his employees who could ever get away with that. She was more like a nagging grandmother to him than one of his staff members, and often times she was the only one who could get through to him. But not today. Not this time.

"Fine. I'll do some research and make sure you have a highly experienced nanny ready to go. Just send me your travel details, and I'll get to work."

Tristan smiled slightly. "Thanks. I knew I could count on you."

Rita winked. "Always."

CHAPTER 2

$\mathcal{D}$aisy's mind swirled with all of the information that Lydia Maynard had shared at the meeting. It seemed that blocking the mall was becoming more and more of a lost cause as the days passed.

"Are you sure there aren't some burial grounds that will be disturbed if they build this mall?" Daisy asked as she followed Lydia to the folding table that held after meeting snacks and coffee.

"Nothing that our attorneys have found. Short of a miracle, it looks like this mall is going to get built. The Aster family is willing to sell them the land, and the city is willing to issue the permits."

Daisy sighed. If anyone could block something like this from happening, it was Lydia. She was about ten years older than Daisy, and her family had been pillars of the community for generations. If

Lydia was throwing in the towel, things must have been bad.

"Okay, maybe we're coming at this from the wrong angle," Daisy said, holding her index finger in the air.

"What do you mean?" Lydia took a long sip of the now room temperature coffee.

"Maybe there's nothing we can do legally, but what if we implore the company buying the land? What if we beg? What if we explain how much this town means to us?"

Lydia laughed. "Seriously? Do you honestly think the billionaire - yes, an actual billionaire - that owns the company cares what we think? Come on, Daisy."

Daisy put her hand on her hip. "Well, I'm glad I don't give up as easily as you do. What if I give him a call? Just to put out some feelers? He's a human being. Surely he has a heart and can understand how much this means to our town."

"That's fine, but I think it's a waste of time." Lydia reached for her briefcase and pulled out a piece of paper. "This is the name of the man who owns the company."

Daisy stared down at the paper and smiled. "I'm going to fix this. I just know I can reason with this guy. I have a good feeling about it."

Lydia rolled her eyes. "Ever the optimist, Daisy Davenport."

~

As she sat at her heavy oak breakfast table, Daisy rolled the edge of the paper down between her fingers. She'd been procrastinating for days now. What was she going to say to this guy?

The meeting had gotten her so pumped up that she could barely think straight when she told Lydia she was going to make that call. Now she was regretting her life decisions.

After all, she wasn't exactly a negotiator. The most negotiating she'd ever done was at the yearly Thornhill flea market, and even then she never got a great deal. She didn't like confrontation, and she hated debating, so what in the world made her think she could talk this guy out of making millions of dollars from putting a mall in her small town?

She stared down at the paper again. Tristan Spencer. He even sounded rich. And probably snobby and cut-throat. And scary. Ugh.

"Just do it, Daisy," she whispered to herself. Good thing she lived alone or someone might think she was losing her mind. She picked up her cell phone for the tenth time that morning, but this time she finally dialed the number.

"Tristan Spencer's office. How can I help you?" a pleasant woman said from the other end of the line. Daisy took in a deep breath.

"Um, yes, hi. I'm looking for Tristan Spencer, please."

"I'm sorry, but he's out of town at the moment."

"Oh. Well, it's very important that I speak with him..."

"Are you the nanny, by chance? The temp agency assured me someone would be at the beach house this afternoon. Tristan will be very upset if you aren't there on time."

Daisy froze in place. The nanny? Beach house? She'd taken one semester of theatre in high school, but was now really the time to use that not fully developed skill?

"Yes. I *am* the nanny. I just need the address to the beach house."

The woman paused for a moment, and then Daisy heard papers rattling in the background. "I sure hope you're not too far from January Cove, young lady. Being late is one of Tristan's pet peeves. He may fire you right there on the spot if you're not there by three o'clock sharp."

"Of course. I will have plenty of time to spare," Daisy said, furiously opening her laptop to Google where January Cove was. Please God, let it still be in the state of Georgia, she thought. It was about three hours away, but if she left soon, she could make it in time.

The woman rattled off the address and hung up. Daisy sat there for a moment, trying to catch her breath. What was she doing? So she was going to drive to a city she didn't know a thing about to confront a man who didn't know her from Adam's house cat. This wasn't going to end well.

~

As Tristan drove into January Cove, he glanced back at his daughter who was sleeping soundly in the back seat. The drive from Atlanta had been about four hours, and Elliana had chattered away for most of that time.

She talked about school and dance classes and how she missed Tatiana. Tristan listened intently, but his mind was also bouncing around, trying to keep up with business deals. Without a nanny to pick up the slack, he had no idea how he would make it through the summer. Hopefully Rita had someone lined up to meet them in January Cove.

This was one of those quaint little beach towns that people loved, but for him it was just another place to work. Although he loved the beach, he rarely put his feet in the sand. Normally, he just worked on his laptop on the balcony overlooking whatever body of water was in front of him.

This time it was a place that the locals apparently called "Billionaire Beach". A small stretch of land on the edge of January Cove, the area boasted some of the most expensive homes in all of coastal

Georgia. "Nothing but the best" was Tristan's motto. He wasn't about to make his daughter spend the summer in some tiny cottage near the water.

Although he didn't want to raise a daughter with a silver spoon in her mouth, he also wanted his constant working to mean something. He wanted a stable future for her, and making as much money as possible was the way to do that.

He pulled up to the guard gate and held up his ID. "Tristan Spencer. We're staying in the Lafayette House."

The guard smiled and nodded. "Yes, sir. We've been expecting you." The gate opened as the guard handed Tristan a set of keys. "It's the light blue one at the end of the street. Enjoy your stay, sir."

"Oh, one more thing," Tristan said. "A temporary nanny will be joining us later today. I don't know her name, honestly, but when she arrives can you point her in the right direction?"

"Of course, sir."

"Thanks."

As he drove down the short road, Tristan could smell the sea air already. He had to admit that something about the ocean calmed him a bit, but it wasn't enough to keep him from fuming about the continual interference of environmentalists on his projects lately.

The one in Thornhill was, pun intended, a thorn in his side. The little town was perfect for the mall development, but some days he wondered if it was all worth it. Many people in the town didn't want the sprawling commercial development to be built, but it was the perfect location and price.

"Are we here?" Elliana asked, bleary eyed from her long nap.

"Yes, we are, sweetie." Tristan pulled into the stone paved driveway and parked his luxury SUV.

"Can we go to the beach now?" she asked, excitedly.

"Maybe a little later. I have some calls to catch up on, and we need to unpack."

"Daddy..."

He turned around in his seat. "Just a few calls, El. Then I'm all yours for the rest of the evening, okay?"

The disappointed look on her face was one he was becoming all too familiar with, but he had to push the guilt away and do what was best for his business. After all, a successful business would give his daughter the best future. At least that's what he told himself.

Daisy drove through the quaint little beach town. It was a nice place, but she tried to avert her eyes from the vast ocean on the right side of the road. Something about the ocean scared her, most likely because she'd only visited once as a kid.

She remembered vividly how the tide sucked her out too far, and she flailed in the water until her grandfather rescued her. She had no desire to even dip her toes back in the salty water any time soon.

She pulled up to a large guard gate, and her heart started thumping harder. How was she going to get past security?

"Can I help you, ma'am?"

"Oh, um, yes. I'm here to see Tristan Spencer. I'm..."

"The nanny? Yes, he told me you'd be arriving today. He's staying in the blue house at the end of this road. It will have a sign that says Lafayette House."

Daisy's hands trembled as she gripped the steering wheel. "Great. Thanks." She slowly drove through the open passageway as the gate opened for her.

She never did things like this. The most trouble she'd given her grandparents as a teenager was sneaking out to tip cows with her friends, and now she felt really bad for those cows. That was as rambunctious as she had gotten.

But here she was, in a totally different city, about to confront a man who had more money than everyone in her county combined. What was she thinking pulling a stunt like this?

She pulled her small car into the driveway next to the largest SUV she'd ever seen. As she stepped out and looked up at the black monstrosity, she wondered how much it cost to fill up his gas tank. Probably more than she made in a week at her job at the drug store.

Sea gulls squawked overhead, and she could hear the ocean waves behind the house. The place was like a palace in the sand, with huge windows and baby blue siding. Set up on stilts like a circus performer, it towered over even the nicest homes on the street.

She stepped out of her car, grabbing her backpack. She'd only brought a few days worth of clothing, figuring she'd talk to Tristan and then stay at a local motel before driving back the next day.

The stairs were steep, so she was careful to watch her step as she made her way up to the front door. What was she going to say? *"Oh, hi, I'm from Thornhill. I work at the drug store selling foot pads and fungal cream. Would you please take my advice on not building that multi-million dollar mall in my hometown?"*

Even as her finger lingered over the doorbell, she doubted herself. This was a bad idea. What had she been thinking? She turned to go back down the stairs, hoping to make a beeline out of there, when he opened the door unexpectedly.

"Hello?" he said, his voice deeper than she imagined for some reason. It had a hint of Southern in it, which was surprising to her.

"Oh. Hi. I think maybe I've made a mistake..." she stammered, unsure of what to do or say.

"No, you've come to the right place. You're the nanny, right?" There was a slight smile on his face, once she finally looked up at him. Dear God, he was gorgeous. He looked like he'd been chiseled out of stone by some crew of artistic angels. Aware that her mouth was hanging open and that drool was threatening to free fall off her lips, she closed it and swallowed hard. "Are you alright?"

"What? Oh yes. Sorry."

"You're the nanny, right?" he repeated.

She should have said no. She knew she should have said no. All the people in the world shouted in her head and said NO. But did she say no? Nope.

"I am. That's right."

He smiled, cocking his head to the side. "And your name is..."

"Oh. Sorry. Right. You'd want to know my name. I mean that makes total sense."

He stared at her, his smile fading. "Listen, I thought the agency was sending me an experienced nanny, and I have to say that you seem either a bit nervous or possibly high on drugs."

Daisy's eyes opened wide. "Drugs? Oh my gosh! No, of course not! I mean, I've only had maybe five glasses of wine in my entire life. I would never take drugs. Really."

"So you're just not experienced then?"

She paused for a moment, unsure of how to get out of the mess she'd already gotten herself in. "Actually, it's just that I've had a long drive, and I think my blood sugar might be a bit low."

A look of concern spread across his face. "I'm sorry. Please come in. My daughter is out picking up seashells, so I need to go check on her. There are some bananas on the breakfast bar if you'd like a snack to help your blood sugar."

She followed him inside and took a deep breath. If she didn't get her act together, her chances of getting close to him and changing his mind about the mall project were gone.

Her anxiety didn't stop her from noticing the amazing decor inside the home. Although it was a beach house, it didn't look like one. Ornate gold mirrors, white marble floors and the most luxurious furniture she'd ever seen overwhelmed her senses as she walked through the large foyer and into the living room.

"I'm just going to step onto the deck to check on my daughter. Please wait here, if you don't mind."

He pointed to the breakfast bar stool and walked past her onto the deck, closing the door behind him. For the first time in minutes, she took a full breath. The further she got into this scheme, the more anxious she felt. What in the world made her think she could pull this off?

She wasn't a good liar. Never had been. Literally

got caught in every lie she'd ever told. And now she was an undercover spy in a billionaire's beach house? *Good plan, Daisy. Good plan.*

A few moments later, Tristan reentered the kitchen and eyed her carefully. "Blood sugar okay?"

Daisy nodded. "False alarm, I guess."

"Look, I'm not trying to be rude, but are you sure you're up for this?"

"Absolutely. I'm sorry I was so scattered before, Mr. Spencer. I'm not normally like that. I'm a professional, and I'm looking forward to helping you with your daughter while you're on vacation."

His face softened, which told her she was getting through to him. "I'm willing to give you a chance, but please know that I have no patience for unprofessionalism. I expect the best when it comes to Elliana. That's my daughter's name."

"It's beautiful."

"Well, she's beautiful, and smart and sassy and the light of my world."

"How old is she?"

He cocked his head slightly. "I would've thought your agency would have told you. She's eight."

At least she wasn't wearing diapers. "Great age." Daisy had no idea if it was a great age or not. She was just grasping at straws at this point.

Elliana ran into the kitchen and over to her father. She was a cute little girl with long, dark hair that was currently damp from playing at the water's edge, no doubt. Her feet were sandy, and she was wearing a pink sundress that looked like it came out of a kids' fashion magazine or something.

"Elliana, this is... I still don't know your name..."

"Daisy."

"This is Daisy," he said, his voice softening as he spoke to his daughter. "She'll be your temporary nanny while we're here in January Cove for the next couple of months."

Daisy's heart stopped for a moment. Couple of months? She had about three days worth of clothes and no plans to stay any longer than that.

"Hi," the little girl said, barely looking up at her. Elliana turned to her father. "I miss Tatiana."

"Who's Tatiana?" Daisy asked.

"Hey, El, why don't you run upstairs and unpack your things?" The little girl trotted up the stairs without looking back. "Sorry about that. Tatiana was her nanny for a couple of years and just quit without warning to marry her new boyfriend."

"Oh. Wow. Yikes."

"Yeah, so Elliana is having a tough time adjusting to someone new. I hope you're okay with that."

"Of course! Don't give it a second thought. I'm sure it will all work out fine." Even as she said it, she didn't believe it. Two months was still ringing in her head. How in the world was she going to stay there that long without losing her job back home? Her boss, Stanley, wasn't exactly the type to give her that much time for vacation.

"So the agency said I could pay you directly to make things easier. I went ahead and paid them their share. Did they explain your weekly rate?"

"Actually, no. Not really."

"Here, I wrote down some figures. Take a look and make sure you're on board," he said, handing her a notepad from a nearby end table.

She stared down at it, trying desperately not to dance a jig. "So this is the monthly rate?" she asked, pointing to a number larger than what she made in a couple of months.

Tristan laughed loudly. "No, of course not! I'm not a scrooge, Daisy. That's your weekly pay."

She needed a brown paper bag because it sure felt like she was about to hyperventilate. He was paying her that much *per week*? If she worked the whole summer, she would be financially free in two months and maybe even have enough to put down on her first home.

"Really?"

"I know it's a bit more than what you'd expect, but I will need your full-time job to be tending to Elliana. I work a lot, probably more than I should, and I want to know that my daughter is in good hands. Are we in agreement?"

She swallowed hard, still trying not to jump up

and down like she'd won the lottery. "Absolutely. I look forward to a wonderful summer."

He reached out and shook her hand, his large fingers wrapping around hers. His hand was warmer than she'd imagined.

"I hate to leave you standing here, but I'm actually late for a conference call. The fridge is fully stocked, so if you can take some time to plan tonight's dinner, that would be great. I should be back down in half an hour or so."

Dinner? Oh no, he expected her to cook? She wasn't a cook. She could barely boil an egg. Oh, who was she kidding? She had never boiled an egg in her life. If it didn't come in a box with a peel off plastic sheet that you had to poke with a fork to microwave it, she didn't cook it.

"Great. I'll do that."

He started up the stairs, but turned back to her. "Oh, and your room is up the stairs, second door on the left, just across from mine. Settle in when you're ready."

She watched him walk up the stairs and into a room, shutting the door behind him. Finally, she could let out the breath she'd been holding. She dropped her backpack and squealed quietly to herself, throwing her arms in the air like a crazed cheerleader.

Her excitement was quickly squelched by the sound of someone tapping on the front door. She walked over and pulled on the large, wrought iron knob.

A young woman was standing there, several suitcases beside her, a big smile painted across her face. She looked pristine, like someone had dressed her for the part of "perfect secretary with bun".

"Can I help you?" Daisy asked.

"Hello. I'm Charlotte Dempsey, the nanny. My agency sent me. Is Tristan Spencer here?"

Oh no. The real nanny. This woman could singlehandedly foil her plans and possibly get her arrested for impersonating someone else.

"I'm sorry, but there must be some sort of mistake. We're in no need of a nanny here," Daisy said as she started to shut the door. The woman reached out and pushed against it slightly.

"But my agency sent me. Here are my orders," she said, holding out a sheet of paper. Daisy pretended to look at it.

"Oh, I know what happened. My fiancé, Tristan, must have thought he needed someone because I wasn't originally able to come on this trip. But my plans changed last minute. You see, my European tour was rescheduled because my drummer... Derek... got the chicken pox of all things. Can you believe that luck? Anyway, so I'm here now, and we don't need a nanny this summer. But, hey, you look great, and I'm sure someone will hire you in a jiffy. Sorry about the mixup. You know men. They forget things sometimes..." Daisy said as she shut the door, leaving poor Charlotte standing there with her mouth hanging open.

She leaned against the door for a moment, hoping Tristan hadn't overheard any of their exchange. Then she peeked out the window and watched the woman drive away, looking back at the house as she went.

Suddenly, a flurry of worries flew through Daisy's head. What if the guard told Tristan that two nannies had shown up? What if the agency called him?

This was getting way too complicated. But now she was in it way too deep to get out. And then there was the money. There was no way she was giving up the opportunity to make that kind of money. So, against her better judgment, she'd keep up this charade and ride it 'til the wheels fell off. Her town, and her bank account, depended on it.

CHAPTER 3

$\mathcal{M}$ egan sat quietly on the other end of the line for several moments. "Have you lost your mind? Like, seriously, do I need to call someone?"

"I'm questioning that myself," Daisy whispered into the phone. She'd settled into her room after doing some basic meal planning. So far, she'd come up with tacos or hamburgers, and neither of those options sounded very impressive for her new boss. "But I'm in too deep right now, and I need your help."

"How can I help?"

"First, I need you to call Stanley and make up any story you can to get me the next two months off."

"*Two months*? You are crazy. I need to call the closest asylum…"

"I don't think they have asylums anymore, but that's neither here nor there. Look, I know this is going to work. I'll just make friends with this guy and get him to change his mind about Thornhill."

"And what if he finds out who you really are?"

"He won't."

"But what if he does?"

"Then I'll run as fast as possible to my car and disappear from the planet."

"Yeah, that sounds like a plan." She could almost hear Megan rolling her eyes through the phone line.

"Oh, I also need clothes. I only brought three days worth."

"You're kidding me, right?"

"I didn't exactly know I was supposed to stay here the whole summer."

"How am I supposed to get you that many clothes?"

"I actually don't need that many. I mean, it's summer time, so people don't wear much around here. Just go by my place and pack up a bunch of sundresses, shorts, tank tops, that kind of thing. Oh, and a couple of swimsuits. They're in a box in the top of my closet. I like the pink one and that mint green one with the pineapples. Ship them overnight to this address," Daisy said quickly, worried that she'd get caught anytime now. She gave Megan the address of a local mail store she'd found online. The last thing she needed was a big box being delivered to her new employer's beach house. That wouldn't look suspicious at all. Yeah, right.

"And you're sure you want the pineapple one? You said it made your butt look big."

"Big butts are in style now, so I'm good."

Megan chuckled. "I can't believe Daisy Davenport is working as an undercover agent in the home of one of the richest men in America. What could possibly go wrong with this plan?"

"Very funny. I'm going to make this work."

"And the fact that you don't know the first thing about kids or have any idea how to cook?"

"Just minor details."

Tristan stared out over the vast expanse of water. His balcony overlooked the deserted, private beach behind the house. This space was reserved for just him and his daughter for the entire summer. Well, and the new nanny. The quirky, very attractive, but very strange new nanny.

She wasn't at all what he'd expected. Tatiana had been polished, proper and all about the business of taking are of Elliana, which is what he'd wanted. But this Daisy woman was different. A little rough around the edges. A little nervous. It made him wary, but intrigued. And Tristan Spencer didn't get intrigued often.

Maybe that was why he'd gotten along with Tatiana so well. She was there to care for his daughter, but she didn't interfere in his world. She stood back and allowed him to be absent. She took up the slack, or so he'd hoped. There was a part of him that wanted Elliana to love her so he felt less guilty about working so much.

"Daddy?" Elliana said from behind him.

"Oh, hey, sweetie. I didn't know you were standing there."

She walked over and sat down on the end of his bed. "Is that lady always going to be my nanny?"

Tristan smiled. "No, honey. She's just here for the summer until we can find someone new."

Elliana sighed and looked down at her feet. "I hate having a nanny."

Tristan's heart caught in his chest. "What? Why?" He knelt in front of her and met her eyes.

"Because having a nanny means I don't have you."

Before he could say anything, she stood up and walked slowly out of the room, still hanging her head. As he listened to her shut the door to her bedroom, he'd never felt like such a failure in his life.

Daisy stood in the kitchen, staring at the appliances like she'd just landed on another planet. Her kitchen at home was what one might call basic. Microwave, avocado green stove from the seventies - with only one working burner - and a matching green refrigerator that had a smell no matter how many times she cleaned it.

But this place was unlike anything she'd ever seen. Double wall ovens with shiny stainless steel, a huge island covered in light colored granite with flecks of gold in it, a bunch of burners that looked like something from a restaurant and several smaller countertop gadgets she couldn't identify.

She opened a few drawers, desperate to find owners' manuals, but nothing. Not one thing to help her operate these appliances. No cookbooks. Just a kitchen that looked like something from a magazine and a nanny that looked like someone from Mars who had no idea how Earth worked.

It wasn't too late to run. The idea flashed through her mind. How bad was a mall, anyway? Women loved malls, right?

Not her. She just couldn't do it. She had to fight or else her grandparents would probably haunt her forever.

"Settling in okay?" Tristan asked as he quietly walked up behind her. She twirled around quickly, pasting a fake smile on her face.

"Yes. I've unpacked, and I was just familiarizing myself with the kitchen."

Tristan's nose turned up slightly as he looked

around. "It's not much, but hopefully you can make it work."

"Not much?" She almost swallowed her tongue.

"Well, the kitchen in my house is about twice this size with a few more bells and whistles, but this will do for the summer."

Bells and whistles? What kinds of bells and whistles did this man have? Were there butlers? Did someone wipe his mouth after each bite? Was there a robot that cooked his meals? She tried to imagine what life was like with a billion dollar bank account. She couldn't even imagine what life was like with a five thousand dollar bank account.

"It will work just fine. I did want to do a little meal planning, so I may need to run to the grocery store..."

"Of course. Here's my card," he said, reaching into his wallet and handing her a black card. A black card. Who had one of those? "The closest market is just around the corner. They don't do delivery, unfortunately."

"No problem. I like going grocery shopping," she said without thinking. What she really meant was she liked going to the grocery store and buying frozen meals and pre-made subs, but he didn't need to know her personal eating habits.

"Really? That sounds like the worst activity in the world." He really was a snooty, she thought.

"Well, I'll get going then. I need a few things for dinner."

"Take the golf cart. It's under the house in the carport." He tossed her some keys off the island.

"Golf cart?"

"It's the easiest way to travel around here, from what I'm told. Do you need me to crank it?"

Daisy cocked her head and chuckled. "No, sir. I think I can manage." How many tractors and lawn-mowers had she driven on her grandparents' property in her life? Certainly, she could operate a golf cart.

She turned to walk toward the front door. "Excuse me?" he said, his tone sharp.

"Yes?" she asked, turning around.

"You are taking Elliana with you, right?"

"Oh. Right. Of course. Sorry about that." How in the world was she going to remember this kid? First off, she wasn't a kid person. She could take them or leave them, and in this case, she had planned to leave her.

"Elliana? Come on down and ride to the store with Daisy."

"Who's Daisy?" Elliana yelled back. Tristan sighed and walked up the stairs to talk to his daughter in private. Moments later, they both appeared in front of Daisy, the little girl pouting with her arms crossed.

"Sorry about that. She just has to get used to you."

Daisy forced a smile. "No problem. Come on, Elliana. I'm sure we can find you some great snacks at the store."

"I doubt it," Elliana said, rolling her eyes. She begrudgingly followed Daisy out the front door and down the stairs as Tristan watched from the porch.

Daisy was keenly aware that he was watching, so she quickly turned around and engaged Elliana in conversation.

"So, have you been to this beach before?" she asked, smiling broadly as they rounded the corner to the carport.

"No," Elliana responded sharply.

They were now out of Tristan's sight, so Daisy didn't feel the need to put on a show. She climbed into the golf cart as Elliana did the same on the other side. She turned the key, relieved to hear it beep. The last thing she needed was Tristan thinking she was too dumb to operate a golf cart.

She decided to make a half circle in and drive out of the driveway forward. Instead, she underestimated the sensitivity of the gas pedal and sent them careening at full speed through the open back of the carport and right into a large sand dune next to the pool. Thank God they didn't end up *in* the pool.

Elliana screamed, which sent Tristan running down the back steps.

"Are you okay?" he yelled as he ran closer.

"We're fine," Daisy called back, after checking to see if Elliana was in one piece. "This wonderful sand dune saved us from a swim in the pool."

Tristan looked ticked off, his face red and rigid. Apparently, he didn't see the humor in this kind of situation. Duly noted.

"El, are you alright?" he asked his daughter. She nodded and rolled her eyes, before crossing her arms over her chest again. "Can I speak with you for a moment, Daisy?" he said, through gritted teeth.

Daisy slowly followed him to the other side of the pool, her head hanging in embarrassment.

"Do I need to call the agency and request someone else?"

His tone was firm. The last thing she needed was for him to call the agency and find out she wasn't even the right nanny. Actually, she wasn't even a nanny at all.

"No, sir. I'm so sorry. I didn't realize how sensitive the gas pedal was, and I just pressed too hard. But now I know, and I'll be very careful."

"The whole reason you're here is to take some of the stress off of me as it relates to taking care of my daughter."

His sentence hit Daisy wrong. Taking care of his own daughter caused him stress? What a tool.

"I understand," Daisy said without looking at him.

He paused and sucked in a sharp breath. "Good. Please be careful going to the store." With that, he walked back into the house and slammed the French doors that led to the deck.

Daisy slowly slid back into the seat of the golf cart and sighed. "Sorry I scared you."

"You didn't scare me," Elliana said under her breath.

She was as tough as her father.

Daisy and Elliana pulled up to the grocery store. It looked similar to the one in her beloved town of Thornhill, a place she was desperately missing right now. January Cove was beautiful, no doubt, but she was doing all of this for the good of Thornhill. She thought about the looks of gratitude on the faces of her fellow townspeople. Surely, they would be excited if the mall deal was squashed. She'd be a hero.

"*This* is the grocery store?" Elliana said, her upper lip pulled up like she'd smelled something bad.

"Yes. Why?"

"Ours is a lot nicer than this one."

Ugh. Rich kids were hard to deal with, she thought to herself.

She wouldn't know anything about being rich. Life had always been challenging for her and her family. Struggle was something that Daisy knew well. Before her mother had died when she was nine years old, she'd watched the life of a drug addict from her front row seat. Constant moving, electricity being turned off, staying in motels in the seediest areas of town.

When she was Elliana's age, she'd seen her mother overdose at least six times, and this grocery store in January Cove would've looked like the Taj Mahal to her.

"I think it's a nice grocery store, actually," Daisy said as she pulled the keys out of the ignition. "Let's go."

She was already done with this kid, and it hadn't even been three hours. How was she going to do this for two whole months?

They got a small cart and started walking through the brightly lit store. They had a little of everything from eggs and cheese to boogie boards and floats. Such was a beach town grocery store.

"Do you like pancakes?" Daisy asked as they perused the aisles.

"I guess so."

"Great," Daisy said, ignoring the little girl's tone. "What about eggs."

"Gross."

"Does your Dad like eggs?"

"I don't know."

"Don't you eat breakfast with him?" Daisy asked, stopping in the aisle.

Elliana laughed out loud. "My Dad leaves for the

office at five in the morning. We never eat breakfast together. Tatiana would make me breakfast."

"And she would eat with you?"

"Sometimes. Usually, she just made it and I ate by myself."

For some reason, that made Daisy a little sad. "What about cereal?"

Elliana shrugged her shoulders. "I like the chocolate ones."

"Good. We'll get some of those." She got a hint of a smile from Elliana, and that was progress.

Daisy fell face first onto her bed, her arms stretching across it. This had been the most exhausting day of her life. Kids were hard work, even if they were someone else's kid.

After their grocery trip, she'd come back to the house, put away the groceries, took Elliana to collect seashells on the beach, cooked dinner - thanks to Google and an easy spaghetti recipe she'd found - served dinner to Elliana on the deck and taken a plate to Tristan in his office.

This guy didn't even take a break to eat dinner with his daughter. What was wrong with his priorities?

Obviously, he was in his office concocting plans for the mall project. At least, that's what she imagined in her head. He seemed to have little personality and no empathy for those around him, including his little girl. How was she supposed to get him to feel sorry enough for her and her little town to squash his multi-million dollar project?

It all seemed futile right now.

But she'd made this decision, and she had to follow through with it. After all, she didn't know what the legalities were of pretending to be the nanny and getting caught.

Now that Elliana had gone to bed for the night, she could take some time for herself. She rolled onto her back and stared up at the ceiling fan. She missed home. She missed her warm bed and her view of the pasture, although the beach wasn't that bad as long as she didn't have to get near the water.

Just as she was thinking about putting on her pajamas and watching a sappy movie, she heard a knock at her door. She dragged herself from the plush mattress and walked across the room.

She opened the door to find Tristan standing there, still wearing his button up dress shirt and slacks. Did this guy ever loosen up?

"Yes?"

"Sorry to bother you after hours, but I think we need to talk. Can you meet me on the deck?"

"Oh. Sure. I'll be there shortly."

She closed the door and leaned against it, her

heart rattling her sternum. What did he want to talk about? Did he find out who she really was?

Her hands were shaking, but she managed to take a drink from her water bottle and suck in some deep breaths before heading downstairs. She just wanted to get this over with. Images of police officers waiting for her outside zoomed through her head.

Instead, she found Tristan sitting in one of the Adirondack chairs, a glass of wine in his hand. She sat down in a chair across from him, her back to the ocean. It was already dark, but she could still hear the roar of the waves as they flowed in and out. For many, that was a soothing sound. To her, it was pretty terrifying.

"So, I'd like to talk about Elliana."

"Okay..."

"First, I think you should know that Elliana's mother passed away in a car accident when she was four years old."

"Oh, wow. I'm so sorry. I lost my mother when I was nine and..."

"My condolences. Anyway..." *Wow, what a rude guy.* "As you can imagine, this makes her a bit vulnerable when it comes to close relationships with women."

"I'm not sure what you mean..."

He leaned forward and put his glass down on the table between them, resting his elbows on his knees. His gaze made her feel uncomfortable. She couldn't help but notice how attractive he was, but his jerkiness definitely balanced that out.

"I mean that she has gotten close to women in the past, and when they leave her, she's devastated."

"But I'm only here for two months. I'm not sure what I can do to prevent that from happening. I mean, I'm a pretty lovable person." As soon as she said it, she wanted to reel it back in like a fishing line. She thought she saw a quirk of a smile on his face, but it quickly went away.

"I'm sure you are, Miss Davenport. And quite humble as well."

She bit her lip to keep from laughing at her own comment. "I'm sorry. I was just trying to lighten the mood."

"When it comes to my daughter, I'm very serious. I want you to be a great nanny to her, but I don't want you to form a personal relationship. Once we're back home, I'll be interviewing nannies for long-term work. I need her to connect with them."

"Of course."

"The expectation here is that you'll keep her occupied and safe this summer and make sure she has an enjoyable time. She's been looking forward to this trip for awhile now." He leaned back and started drinking his wine again.

"With all due respect, I think she was looking forward to spending time with her father most of all. Do you intend to spend time with her?"

A flash of anger landed on his face. He sat the glass down once again and leaned forward. "Excuse me? You just met me and Elliana. What would you know about our relationship?" Defensive was an understatement.

"Please don't be offended. It's just that Elliana said something to me in the grocery store today, and it made me think she's missing you."

He sighed and ran his fingers through his hair. "I have a very demanding business, Miss Davenport. I don't get to spend as much time with Elliana as I want. But it's for her future. One day, she'll understand all that I did was for her."

Daisy stood up, unsure of whether their conversation was officially over or not. She started walking toward the French doors, but turned around. "For both of your sakes, I hope you're right."

CHAPTER 4

Tristan stood on his balcony, watching Elliana build a sandcastle. He remembered the times when they would build them together on vacation. She was just a toddler back then, but her artistic skills were that of a genius, at least in his unbiased opinion.

As he watched her move, he marveled at how she'd grown. It seemed like the days and years were passing faster all the time, like a snowball getting bigger and bigger as it rolled downhill. He wanted time to stand still for just a little while, or at least enough time for him to catch up. He supposed all parents felt that way, wanting to hang on to every moment of their children growing up. If money could've bought that, he would have gladly paid up.

He glanced over at Daisy, who was sitting on the deck, intently watching Elliana as well. But he'd noticed that she didn't go on the beach much, and she never went near the water. He wondered what that was about, but it wasn't important as long as she took care of his daughter.

Their conversation a few nights before still made him uneasy. The way that she'd gotten right to the point about Elliana missing him made him angry, even though he knew she was likely right.

It was a catch-22. To run a billion dollar company meant working harder than anyone else would ever imagine. It meant pouring every drop of sweat, blood and occasional, secret tears into his business. But it also meant there was little left over for his daughter, and that made him question everything.

He'd never expected to be a single parent. That wasn't the deal he'd made with Elliana's mother, Kate, all those years ago. Even when they'd divorced, it was fairly amicable, and she'd been a great co-parent. Her dedication to their daughter had allowed him the time he needed to build his business without making Elliana feel left behind. His weekends with her were full of fun back then. Kate had stood in the gap and made things seem normal for their daughter. That was, until she was just gone. In an instant. In one violent moment of cars hitting each other, metal collapsing and glass flying all over the road.

And then he was left to pick up the pieces of his daughter's shattered heart.

Dating hadn't been successful for him either. If

he didn't have time for his precious child, how would he possibly have time for a woman in his life? And each time he'd tried to date, women had either been gold diggers or unwilling to play third fiddle to his business and child.

First, there was Delina. She was Italian and hot headed and not kid friendly. Then there was Shanna, a part-time cocktail waitress and full-time gold digger. When he'd found her information on a sugar daddy website, stating that she was seeking a wealthy man to "help her keep up with her standard of living", he'd ended their short relationship quickly.

Finding a quality woman to share his life with was hard enough, but finding someone who cared about his daughter and was a good role model had proved impossible. Money could buy a lot, but it could also make the water so murky that knowing someone's intentions was almost impossible until it was too late. So, he never let it become too late. He never got close enough that someone could hurt his daughter.

There were days, if he was being honest, that he wondered if he was the biggest perpetrator of hurting Elliana. He saw that look in her eyes, the one where she was pleading for his attention. He told himself that she was okay right now. She was just eight years old. She wouldn't remember this time in her life when she was older. It was more important for him to be there when she was a teenager, so he'd work hard now to make sure that happened.

He told himself all kinds of lies that helped him sleep at night.

His eyes moved back to Daisy again. She smiled and clapped as Elliana danced around in front of her sand castle, showing off the twirls she was learning at her dance classes back home. When was the last time he went to her dance class? Tatiana had gone to the last recital when he'd had to leave town for a business meeting.

The guilt ate at him every single day, but not enough to stop him from working so much. People often told him that being a billionaire was supposed to free him up so that everyone around him did the hard work and he could just sit back, filling up his bank account. But that wasn't the case for Tristan. He had to work harder than anyone around him. It was just his make up. It was how he'd always been.

Daisy glanced up and caught him looking at her. He smiled slightly and threw up his hand, waving first at her and then at Elliana.

"Hey, Daddy! Come down and build a sandcastle with me," she called up to him.

"We'll do that soon, sweetie. I have a conference call in five minutes."

Elliana's face fell slightly before she shrugged her shoulders. As he walked back inside, Daisy caught his eye again. She was on her phone now, covering the mouthpiece so no one could hear her. She was an odd one, that was for sure. And in that moment, the hair on the back of his neck started to rise. This woman wasn't going to get the chance to hurt his child. He needed to watch her closer and figure out what her deal was.

Daisy covered the phone with her hand as she saw Tristan go back inside and shut the door to his room. "Megan, what's going on? I'm not really in a place I can talk."

"I just wanted to update you. I sent you a package of clothes overnight, so they should be there tomorrow. And I spoke to Stanley. I told him you were doing an internship in environmental studies for the summer."

"You're kidding, right? He bought that?"

"Come on, Daisy. He's never been the sharpest knife in the drawer. He only got the drug store because his father died last year."

"True. Listen, thanks, Meg. I couldn't do all of this without you."

"So how's it going?"

"It's okay. This guy is watching me like a hawk, though. One slip up, and I'm toast."

"Just breathe. You're doing fine."

"You said I was crazy and needed mental help,"

Daisy said, chuckling quietly as she watched Elliana dance around again.

"Well, you are crazy. But I love you, and it's my job to keep you calm so you don't end up in jail."

Daisy gasped. "You don't really think I could go to jail, do you?"

"Um, no. Of course not!" Megan said, her voice going up a couple of octaves.

"This just has to work, Meg. I have to stop that mall project."

In that moment, Daisy looked out at the ocean and Elliana dancing around in front of it and wondered why she was fighting so hard to not move on in her life. But that was a thread that she preferred not to pick at right now.

As the days passed, Daisy was getting used to having Elliana around, even though she never expected to be taking care of a child. She hadn't even been a babysitter when she was a teenager. It wasn't really because she disliked children particularly, but she just never knew what to say to them. She hated all of the baby talk and the silly games. Even as a kid, she was serious. She rode horses, took care of farm animals and focused on her schoolwork. Until she was a teenager, of course.

Then she became a royal pain in the butt to her grandparents.

Right now, she had to play the role of the nanny. And it turned out that Elliana wasn't all that bad. She was just a kid who wanted more time with her father, but unfortunately the couple of times Daisy had broached that subject with Tristan, it hadn't gone well.

So, she decided to just do her job. Collect her paycheck, make sure the kid was safe and then move on with her life once summer was over. Hopefully, in the end, her paycheck and bank account would be fatter and her town would be minus one gross, materialistic shopping mall.

At least that was the goal. Right now, she had no plans as to how she would accomplish that part of her mission. First, she had to focus on taking care of his daughter, keeping the house clean and cooking meals for all of them. And those were the three things she had the least amount of experience with in her life.

Her grandmother had done virtually all of the cleaning growing up. She hadn't had a desire to learn, mainly because she had planned a big future for herself. Even though she didn't want to leave Thornhill now, when she was a teenager she'd planned on leaving home and building a fantastic life for herself.

She had all the childhood dreams that most kids

had of being a doctor or attorney or famous singer. Never mind that she couldn't carry a tune in a bucket.

But as she got older and lost her grandparents, life started smashing her in the face with reality. She realized that dreams didn't mean anything unless she had a plan to accomplish them. Dreams were just wishes. She learned that she had to make goals in order to get anywhere. It had to be measurable, with a time limit. And so far none of her goals had come to pass.

Her goal at the moment was to just stay in Thornhill. She just wanted to keep everything the same because she knew how to live that life. It wasn't the most exciting place on Earth, but it wasn't totally disappointing because she had a lifetime of memories around her all the time. It made her feel safe and comforted.

January Cove hadn't been all bad. As long as she stayed away from the water, she was fairly anxiety free. She had a couple of dicey moments with Elliana wanting to go into the water, but somehow she managed to convince the little girl that she would just sit back on the beach. Of course, if Elliana got in trouble in the water, she had no idea what she was going to do.

Being around Tristan was another story altogether. He was the most reserved person she'd ever met, and she was the exact opposite. Sometimes, he'd eat breakfast with them, usually while checking email on his phone or reading the morning headlines on his laptop. His attention was always split between spending time with Elliana and working. She never got his full attention, and that made Daisy sad when she thought about it.

Elliana would try everything to get him to stop working, even going so far as to spill her orange juice on his phone one morning. Tristan had been remarkably calm about it, driving to the local cell phone store within half an hour to replace it. One of the perks of being so wealthy, she supposed. She'd been using a cracked phone for almost three years now, and sometimes a stray shard of glass would cut her cheek during a conversation.

Most of her days with Elliana were spent going to the bookstore, walking the quaint streets of January Cove and building sandcastles. But she could tell the little girl was getting bored with the same daily activities.

"Where are we going?" Elliana asked as they walked far outside of their normal area.

"Well, I thought maybe you might want to try something new?"

"Like what?"

Daisy smiled as they rounded the corner and she pointed at Twinkle Toes, the local dance studio. Elliana jumped up and down.

"They have dance here?"

"Yes, they do! I called them last night, and they have a great summer camp going on. I thought you might like to join them?"

"I would love that! Can I start right now?"

"Of course. I'll pick you up after lunch. Here's your dance bag," Daisy said, handing her a small pink duffel bag she'd packed with Elliana's clothes. "If you need me, the instructor has my number, okay?"

"Thank you, Daisy!" she said, hugging her around the waist before running inside. Daisy smiled. She'd never expected a hug from Elliana, not after their rocky start. But they were forming a bond, day by day, and she found herself starting to enjoy this adventure after all.

Tristan sat on the lower deck off the kitchen and stared out at the horizon. A half hour between conference calls meant a short moment of peace. He wished his daughter was there to spend it with, but she was gone somewhere with Daisy, apparently.

When he heard the door open behind him, he turned with a smile, expecting to see Elliana. Instead, Daisy stood there alone, a bag of groceries on her hip.

"Oh. Hey."

"Hi. I just grabbed a few quick groceries on the way home. Got that hummus you requested."

"Thanks," he said as he stood up. Something about Daisy intrigued him in a way he didn't like to admit to himself. She was beautiful, in a "girl next door" sort of way. She wasn't like the overly made up women he normally saw in his circles. Instead, she had this easygoing vibe about her, like she wasn't trying to impress anyone. But then he got the feeling that there was a lot he didn't know about her, things that were just brewing right under the surface.

She walked into the kitchen and set the bag on the counter. "The stores around here really don't have a lot of what you want, unfortunately. The manager had never even heard of quinoa. And you can forget caviar." She was funny and quirky, two attributes he'd never really thought about in the women he dated. Probably because they were never funny or quirky.

Tristan chuckled. "I'll survive. Say, where's Elliana? In her room? I thought I might spend a few minutes with her."

"She's at dance camp," Daisy said, a big grin on her face.

Tristan's blood pressure started to rise at a rapid clip. "What?"

"Yeah, I know she misses her dance classes, so I enrolled her in a week long dance camp at Twinkle

Toes. Isn't that the cutest name for a dance studio?" She turned to put up a carton of milk.

"You've got to be kidding me. Please say you're joking." He gripped the edge of the counter and leaned forward.

"What's wrong? I didn't think it'd be a big deal because you're so busy..."

"Excuse me?"

"Look, Elliana was getting bored so..."

"Bored? I pay you a lot of money to make sure she's not bored! Why am I paying you when you're not even watching her all week?"

Daisy looked taken aback, her eyes large. "I'm sorry. I should've cleared it with you first. It's just that there's not a lot going on around here and I..."

"Let me make something extremely clear to you, Miss Davenport," he said, his teeth gritted so hard that she could see his jaw twitching. "My daughter is the most important person in my life. I don't just pass her off to total strangers. You don't have the authority to sign her up for anything. Do you understand?"

Daisy nodded. "Understood."

"Good. Now take me to this dance studio so I can get my daughter."

"Okay." Daisy said, hanging her head a bit.

He followed her down to the carport. She slid behind the wheel of the golf cart as he stood there looking at her, his arms crossed over his chest.

"What are you doing?"

"I'm driving you," she said.

"I'll drive. I've seen your skills."

Daisy sighed and slid across to the passenger side as Tristan took his spot as driver. They pulled out of the driveway and onto the street, the silence only made better by the gentle hum of the golf cart motor.

"Turn right up here," Daisy said as she pointed up ahead.

"You know, my daughter is very impressionable."

"Most kids are," Daisy said in a monotone voice.

"She probably thought you didn't want to spend time with her, which is why she agreed to this dance camp."

"With respect, sir, she was very excited about going. She loves dance."

He turned his head and glared at her. "I know she loves dance. I'm her father."

"Take a left at the dry cleaners up there," Daisy said, turning her attention back to the road. "And, *also with respect*, the only person she thinks doesn't want to spend time with her is you."

Tristan pressed the brake hard, stopping the golf cart in the middle of the road. Thankfully, January Cove didn't exactly have massive amounts of traffic.

"Did we break down?" Daisy asked, leaning her head out the side of the cart and looking around.

"No, we didn't break down," Tristan said,

clenching his jaw. "I stopped because I can't believe you, the nanny we literally just met, said my daughter thinks I don't want to spend time with her."

Daisy stared at him, her eyes wide, but she said nothing.

"Well? What do you have to say for yourself?" Tristan asked, feeling like he was scolding a small child.

Her eyes darted to the side and back, as if she was searching for the right words. "Well... I would say that I stand by my assessment."

Tristan gripped the steering wheel and looked back to the road. "You know, I do the best I can. I know it might seem like I don't want to spend time with Elliana, but that's simply not true. She's my world."

"Excuse me for saying so, Mr. Spencer, but the person you should be explaining this to is your daughter. Quite frankly, she's made a few comments to me that led me to believe she's aching for some quality time with you."

Tristan hated that he knew she was right. His daughter did want more time with him. He knew it was true, yet he was keenly aware that he put his business first more times than not. It was a part of his personality he hated, yet sometimes he felt powerless to change it.

He started driving again, saying nothing to Daisy,

tension building in his jaw as he clenched his mouth shut. What was it about this woman that irked him so much?

"Right here," she said, pointing to the dance studio. He stopped the golf cart and got out, walking over to the large glass window that showed a view of the dance studio itself. He could see a myriad of little girls, all dolled up in tutus and leotards, running and leaping across the floor.

He didn't immediately see Elliana, which made his heart rate speed up a bit. What if somebody had taken her? What if she was sick in some back room, needing her father?

"Where is she?" he finally said, his voice a bit shaky.

"She's right over there, with her hand on the bar."

Tristan turned his head slightly to see Elliana lifting her left leg over and over, her back to the window. As she turned toward her teacher, she smiled broadly and twirled around. He could tell that she was happy there, having a good time with a bunch of new friends, it seemed.

"Would you like for me to go inside and let the teacher know that Elliana won't be returning?" Daisy asked softly.

Tristan took in a deep breath and then slowly released it. "No. I think she's fine." He turned back toward the golf cart, but stopped short of getting in.

"You know, we just met. And I've never even been to this town before."

"Look, I really am sorry, Mr. Spencer. I was thinking about what Elliana would enjoy, and I didn't even consider how you might feel about it. I promise that it won't happen again. I'll consult you on everything involving your daughter."

He looked at her for a moment and then nodded. "Good. That's all I ask."

The ride back to the house was quiet and awkward.

CHAPTER 5

"So he almost fired you?" Megan asked from the other end of the phone. To her, this was like a live soap opera playing out right in front of her. Well, through the telephone line, anyway.

"Yes. It was a close call, for sure. But I used all of my big words and best acting from that one high school class we took, and it worked. For now, at least."

"How are you getting along with Elliana?"

"Good, actually. I like the kid. She's very sweet, a little sheltered, but not a brat, surprisingly. I really thought a billionaire's daughter would be a pain."

"Crap, I've got to go. Dylan's calling me about my work schedule. Call me if you need anything."

"Thanks, Meg. I don't know what I'd do without you."

Daisy pressed end on her phone and set it down on the kitchen counter.

"Who's Meg?" Elliana asked from behind her, startling her.

"What?"

"You said you didn't know what you'd do without her."

"How long have you been standing there?"

"I just walked up. Who's Meg?"

"Well, she's my very best friend back home. Do you have a best friend?"

Elliana smiled. "Yes. Her name is Emmy."

"Emmy and Elliana, huh?"

"Yep!"

"Cool. So, what do you want to do today now that your dance camp is over?"

Elliana climbed up onto one of the bar stools. "Can we go on a picnic down at the beach?"

"I think we can do that," Daisy said with a smile. "Let me make some sandwiches, and we'll do it for lunch. Why don't you go get dressed and I'll call you down when I'm ready?"

"Okay!" Elliana said as she bounded up the stairs.

Daisy walked into the kitchen and opened the refrigerator, looking for the ham she'd bought the day before. As she took out the mayonnaise and mustard, she sensed someone behind her.

"Oh, you scared me," she said when she saw Tristan standing on the other side of the breakfast bar.

"Sorry about that. I was just coming down to make myself some lunch."

"I can do that. What would you like?" Gosh, she hoped he picked something easy because her cooking skills were less than stellar. Before he could answer, Elliana came bounding down the stairs again wearing a blue and white checked sundress and her favorite bright pink flip flops.

"Daddy! Are you coming to lunch with us?" she asked as she jumped up and down, her hands in a praying position.

"Lunch?" Tristan said, a quizzical look on his face.

"Yes, we're having a picnic on the beach!" she said, her level of excitement way too much for the situation, in Daisy's opinion.

"Well..."

"I'm just making your father something for lunch. I'm sure he's very busy today," Daisy said, trying not to sound sarcastic.

Tristan squinted his eyes at her and smiled slightly. "Actually, my morning conference call canceled, so I have some time before my afternoon calls. I think I will join you ladies. I mean, if you don't mind?"

Daisy froze. What had she done? Invited the guy who disliked her immensely to eat lunch and bombard her with questions in front of the big, scary ocean?

Sometimes she just didn't think about what she was saying. She had basically just dared him to spend time with her which was insane since she definitely didn't want to blow her cover. As much as she thought he should spend time with his daughter, she didn't intend to spend time with him herself.

"Oh. Great. I'll just make an extra sandwich or two."

"Here, let me help. Elliana, go upstairs in the linen closet and get that big plaid blanket I saw."

Elliana ran up the stairs, probably trying to figure out what a linen closet was. She was quite sure that the child had plenty of maids and help in their real home. But even more surprising was that Tristan was going to help her make a sandwich. She sure didn't see that one coming.

"The secret to a great ham sandwich is right here," he said as he reached into the refrigerator and pulled out a jar of long pickles that were sliced for sandwiches.

"Really? I wouldn't have taken you for a pickle type of guy."

He stopped and looked at her, a quirk of a smile on his face. "And what does a pickle type of guy look like, generally speaking?"

Why did she keep sticking her foot in her mouth? Had she insulted him by not assuming he liked pickles?

"I mean, I wasn't trying to offend you..."

Tristan started laughing. "Relax, Miss Davenport. I'm just poking a little fun at you. But, seriously, the pickles are what make it good. Slap a couple of these on the sandwiches. I mean, do you even like pickles?"

She was so rattled by his sudden friendliness with her, that she didn't even know if she liked pickles. The answer to the question escaped her for a few moments.

"Yes, I like pickles. I love pickles. I'm a member of the local pickle club back home. "

Again, why was she trying to be sarcastic with this man? Something about him just made her want to dig in her heels and argue, even if it was about pickles.

He smiled again, which was way cuter than she wanted it to be. Most of the time his face looked like a big block of stone that would shatter given the opportunity. But, instead, he looked easy-going as he rolled up the sleeves of his dress shirt and started pulling bread out of the bag.

"I'll have you know that even when I was a kid, I made the sandwiches when we would go on picnics. There is this forest land, you know the type that's protected by the government, and we would have picnics there all throughout the summer..."

As he spoke, she was half listening to his story and half thinking that if he was so into protecting land, why was he destroying her little town? Before too long, she realized that she wasn't paying attention and he was looking at her, as if he was waiting for an answer.

"Are you all right there?"

"What? Sorry. I didn't hear that last part."

"I asked you if you wanted mustard or mayonnaise or both?"

"Oh, just mayonnaise, please. I can do that if you want me to..." she said as she reached for the butter knife. He pulled it back.

"Did you not hear the part about how I'm a master sandwich maker? If you make the sandwiches, you're never going to know just how truly talented I am when it comes to pressing slices of bread together with meat in between. Do you really want to lose out on that kind of an opportunity?"

His face was impassable. She wasn't sure if he was serious or making a joke until he finally let out a chuckle.

"I'll get the bottled water," she finally said, aching to get out of the situation. Did this guy have some sort of personality disorder? How did he flip from being so intolerable to being so dang adorable? This was probably how rich guys got women. They were allowed to act any way they wanted to as long as they had a fat bank account and a nice car.

She pulled the bottled water out of the refrigerator and put it into the cooler that was sitting on the counter. After a few minutes, Tristan had finished the sandwiches and then grabbed a bag of chips and the blanket and headed out the back door of the house.

As they walked towards the ocean, Daisy tried not to let on that she was truly terrified of the water. She wanted no part of it, but the last thing she needed was to alert Tristan to that fact. She was sure that he would wonder why she'd agreed to sign onto a long-term commitment when the house was literally sitting at the edge of the ocean.

Thankfully, he told Elliana not to go too close to the water so that they didn't have as much wind to deal with.

Elliana and Daisy laid out the blanket while Tristan held the cooler and water. Once they got it smoothed out, they all sat down and started digging into the food.

Elliana kept her father's attention for quite some time, regaling him of stories from dance camp and different videos she had been watching on YouTube when there was nothing else to do. It made Daisy happy to see the little girl getting the attention she needed from her father. Shockingly, she hadn't seen him look at his phone one time during their picnic.

After she ate her sandwich, Elliana spied a small dog down by the water's edge with its owner. The older woman waved at them, and Elliana asked if she could go pet the dog. Tristan called to the woman to make sure it was okay and then Elliana took off. This left Daisy completely alone with Tristan and unsure of what to say or do.

"She's a great little girl," she said. Anytime you complimented somebody's kids, it was always a good thing. It immediately endeared them to you. At least that was her theory.

"Yes she is," he said, looking lovingly at his daughter as she giggled at the silly little dog. Tristan then turned his attention back to Daisy. "Look, I want to apologize about my reaction the other day with dance camp. I'm very particular about who I allow around my daughter, and I guess I overreacted a little bit."

He wasn't making eye contact, and she could tell that apologizing wasn't something that he normally did. So, instead of making a multitude of sarcastic remarks that she had ready to go inside her brain, she decided to just let it go.

"It's okay. I mean I don't have kids, but I can imagine that it's difficult when you're a single parent to trust people you don't know."

"Well, anyway, I'm sorry about that."

They sat in silence for a few moments, Daisy

trying not to look at the water, but Tristan staring at it.

"I love the ocean. I've loved it since I was a little kid. Just the in and out of the waves, always bringing something new to the shore. I guess it represents possibilities to me."

What was it with this guy? Now he was a poet? What was she supposed to say to that? That she was terrified of the ocean and all the little gnarly, scary creatures that lurked underneath in the spooky dark water? Yeah, that was great lunch conversation.

"And the house... It's a nice place." That was all she could come up with? When she got home, she was definitely getting a thesaurus. Certainly there had to be more words she could use that didn't make her sound like a middle schooler.

Tristan looked up at the house and then back at her. "Yes, I suppose it's pretty nice for a beach house."

"I guess you're accustomed to much nicer things, huh?"

He smiled slightly. "Money doesn't necessarily buy happiness, Miss Davenport."

What a strange thing to say, she thought. He was a billionaire, and she was quite certain if she had a fat bank account like he did, her worries would be over. No more getting her electricity shut off, no more embarrassment when her card was declined at the local grocery store. Yeah, a billion dollars would make her quite happy.

Elliana ran back to the blanket, coughing a bit after she stopped running.

"Are you okay, sweetie?" Tristan asked, a look of worry on his face.

"Yeah, I just need to take my inhaler, I think," she said. "I left it on the kitchen counter. I'll go get it."

As Elliana trotted back into the house, Tristan watched her. "She has mild asthma. Tatiana took her to the allergist last year and got her tested for me. Sometimes, she reacts to dogs, but not usually."

"I'm sure she'll be fine," Daisy said, trying to sound encouraging.

"You're probably right," he said as Elliana came running back to the blanket.

"I took two puffs like the doctor showed me."

"Good," Tristan said, reaching up and squeezing her cheek. She giggled.

"Stop it, Daddy! I told you I'm too old for that now." She rolled her eyes and smiled.

"You'll never be too old to be my little girl, though," he said, pulling her down onto his lap and playfully biting her neck. She squirmed and laughed, and it warmed Daisy's heart to see their interaction. Up until now, all she'd seen from Tristan was constant stress and the back of his head as he walked upstairs for another phone call. How did he know so many people?

Tristan let her go and laughed as she ran toward the water, cackling at the top of her lungs and taunting him to chase her. Before he could stand up, he reached into his pocket to look at his phone.

"Dang it," he said to no one in particular.

"What's wrong?"

"My afternoon appointment just got cancelled too. Something about a weather event in South America."

"South America?"

"That's where the client lives."

"Oh. I don't think I've ever known anyone outside of North America."

He chuckled. "Really?"

"In fact, I don't know anyone west of Alabama."

Tristan's mouth dropped open. "So you've never traveled?"

She was embarrassed now. "No. I just haven't had the chance yet."

He smiled slightly. "Make it a priority. You'll never regret seeing the Eiffel Tower or the Great Wall of China or even those little hidden beaches on the coast of Greece."

Sure, once she cashed in all of her gold bars, she'd travel the globe, she thought. Sarcasm was her gift.

"I'm sure you're right."

Elliana ran back toward them, stopping at the edge of the blanket. "Why aren't you chasing me?"

"Sorry, sweetie. I was just chatting with Miss Davenport here."

"Miss Davenport? Why don't you call her Daisy?"

Tristan wagged his finger at Elliana. "Sweetie, what have I told you about calling adults by their first names?"

"It's okay. I told her she could call me Daisy."

Tristan eyed her carefully, and then looked back at his daughter. "You may call her Miss Daisy."

Daisy laughed loudly. "Like the movie?"

He looked at her for a moment before letting out a laugh of his own. "Right. Maybe just Daisy is okay."

"What movie?" Elliana asked, her eyebrows furrowed.

"Nevermind. Listen, I just found out I have the rest of the day free, so what would you like to do, El?"

The little girl thought for a moment, her finger tapping her chin as she darted her eyes around. "I know! It's something I've wanted to do for my whole entire life!"

"Your whole entire life, huh? Well, then we have to do it, right?" he looked at Daisy, and she nodded in agreement.

"Of course. I mean, it's her lifelong dream." Tristan smiled at her, and her heart did some kind of flippy flop thing that might have warranted a call to a cardiologist.

"I want to go on a dolphin cruise!"

Daisy heard nothing after that. Everything sounded muffled, like the teacher's voice on a Charlie Brown cartoon. Her vision even started to blur, and everything felt slower. Maybe she needed to see a neurologist too...

"Daisy? Did you hear me?" Tristan asked, touching her arm.

"What? Oh. Sorry. No. What did you say?"

He looked a little concerned. "I asked if you knew where the ferry dock is?"

"Oh. Not exactly. I remember passing it..." She couldn't get it together. How was she going to get out of this dolphin cruise? Surely, this would mean getting on a boat. That was what a cruise was, after all. And there would be water. Lots and lots of dark, scary water with sea creatures she couldn't identify lurking just beneath.

What if she fell overboard? What if something jumped out of the water and snatched her right out of the boat? What if she got seasick? She'd never been on a boat before, so she had no idea if she'd turn green and puke right on Tristan's expensive shorts. Who owned expensive shorts, anyway? Billionaires, that's who.

"I'm so excited! I'm going to change into my dolphin dress!" Elliana said before running straight into the house, leaving the two of them to clean up from the picnic.

"She's a little hyper," Tristan said as they started gathering the trash and tossing it into the basket.

"I can see that."

"You're okay going with us, right?"

Say no. Say no. Say no.

"Of course. Sounds like a great afternoon!"

She was going to die.

CHAPTER 6

*a*s they walked down the pier, Daisy felt her legs trembling. She was certain that they would give way at any moment and send her plummeting to the ocean floor below. Why hadn't she learned to swim? Why had she spent her summers reading books and tending to horses instead of learning to at least doggie paddle?

"You okay?" Tristan asked as they walked, Elliana trotting up ahead, trying to get to the boat before them.

"What? Oh, yeah. I'm great. Couldn't be better."

He laughed. "You're terrified of the ocean, aren't you?"

Daisy stopped in her tracks and looked at him. "Why would you say that?"

"Because you're a terrible liar. Seriously, don't ever play poker." His crooked smile and dimpled cheeks made her feel funny things in her stomach.

77

Or maybe it was the all consuming terror she was feeling as she stood on what appeared to be a very old, very rickety boardwalk teetering over the abyss that was sure to steal her very soul.

Okay, maybe he was right.

"Fine. You're right. I'm scared of the ocean in ways I cannot even describe."

"Then why did you agree to this?"

She sighed and shrugged her shoulders. "Because Elliana is the coolest little girl I've ever met, and I didn't want to let her down."

Something changed in his face. Was it appreciation for what she'd said about his daughter?

"You don't have to go. I can make an excuse if you want."

She thought briefly about his offer. "Trust me, I want to take you up on that. I'd love nothing more than to turn and run straight back to the house right now. But..."

"But?"

"I know I need to overcome this fear."

"Or you could just never come back to the beach?"

She smiled. "That too. But, seriously, I'd like to try. I mean, I think I need to show a good example for Elliana, right?"

He nodded. "That's very admirable. Fear is a hard thing to overcome."

They started walking again. "Oh yeah? And what is the wealthy, successful Tristan Spencer scared of?"

"I didn't say I was scared of anything."

"Come on, slowpokes! The boat is going to leave without us!" Elliana called from up ahead. She was standing at the front of the line, waving past the few other people that were standing behind her.

"Saved by the bell," Daisy mumbled.

As they boarded the boat, Tristan was keenly aware that Daisy was petrified. She carefully stepped over the small gap between the pier and the boat, looking down over and over as if it might swallow her up, even though it was only a couple of inches.

He'd never seen someone so scared of something, and it made him feel bad for her. But it also made him proud to see her facing her fears. He admired it more than she knew, but he definitely wasn't going to tell her that.

"You okay?" he asked quietly as they made their way to the back of the boat and took a seat.

"Are you going to keep asking me that?" she asked, a forced smile on her face.

"I suppose not."

They sat down, and Elliana immediately starting leaning over the side of the boat, looking down into the water below. Daisy grabbed the back of her dress and jerked her into the seat like her life depended on it.

"Hey! Why'd you do that?" Elliana asked, her face both irritated and confused.

"Oh... Sorry, Elliana... I just..."

"Because you didn't read the posted rules over there, sweetie. See where it says no leaning over the railing? You could fall in."

Daisy cut her eyes at Tristan, obviously thankful he didn't tell Elliana about her fear of the ocean.

"Welcome aboard, everyone!" A large, rotund man with a long gray beard appeared on the deck. He was wearing a loud Hawaiian shirt tucked into a pair of shorts that rode way too low, revealing his substantial belly. Topped off by a pair of fisherman sandals and reflective sunglasses, he looked like Santa Claus on vacation.

"Our dolphin cruise this afternoon will last about two hours. Hopefully, we'll see many dolphins. I'd like to invite the kids to come to this side where Susie will lead an educational program about all kinds of sea life in January Cove while the parents can sit back, relax and enjoy some peace and quiet as we ride the waves."

Elliana grinned from ear to ear as she ran to join the handful of other kids. Tristan had to admit he wasn't sad to get to spend some time with Daisy. It'd been a long time since he'd met a woman he could have a conversation with that didn't involve business or money or cocktail parties. She was just normal, and normal was rare for him.

Over the years, he'd learned that the more money he made, the less real people he met. Everyone wanted something from him. They had business proposals, loan requests and he'd even had a few marriage proposals from women whose faces sat right beside the word "gold digger" in the dictionary.

As the boat motor started making noise, Daisy tensed up, her hand gripping the side of the boat tightly, causing the blood to drain from her fingers.

"Can I help you in some way?" Tristan finally asked.

"Why do you think I need help?"

"Because your fingers look like they're about to break off," he said, reaching up and prying her hand from the side of the boat.

She loosened up a bit as the boat started to move. "I can't believe I'm doing this."

"You've never been to the beach before?"

"Once. I was a kid, though. Had a bad experience and almost drowned."

"Oh... well, that makes sense then."

"You could help by distracting me," she said suddenly.

"And how should I do that?"

"Well, first you can answer my question," she

said, a quirk of a smile on her face.

"What question is that?" he asked, knowing full well what it was.

"What scares Tristan Spencer?"

"First of all, it scares me when people call me by my whole name. It's a little weird."

"Funny."

"Second, we don't know each other all that well, so I don't think sharing deep, personal thoughts is appropriate."

"I just shared my biggest fear with you," she said, squinting her eyes at him.

Tristan sighed. "Fine. I'll share one of my fears."

"Okay. What is it?"

"Clowns."

"Clowns? Seriously?"

"A lot of people are scared of clowns. They even make movies about them!"

Daisy giggled. "But they're fun. I mean, they have the big shoes..."

"I *hate* the big shoes."

He watched her smile as he described his lifelong fear of various types of circus performers, all but forgetting her fear of the ocean looming below them.

She started to relax a bit, even looking out onto the water, a peaceful expression on her face. "Is that an island?"

"Yeah, I think there are a couple around here. Uninhabited from what I understand."

"Interesting..." she said as she continued to look around. Elliana was obviously enjoying her time with the other kids, only looking over at them once to quickly wave before becoming immersed in what Susie was saying to the group.

"So, what do you do back home when you're not nannying?" he asked. Daisy froze in place, a look of fear on her face again. "What's wrong?"

"Oh. Nothing. I just felt the boat move funny."

"It's fine. I'm sure Santa over there has done this a million times."

"I hope so. Distract me again. Tell me your most exciting business deal right now."

Tristan cocked his head. "You want to talk about my business deals? Why?"

Her eyes widened. "No reason. I just need something complex to think about right now. You know, to get my mind off worrying that a shark is swimming in circles underneath us right now, smelling the fear that I'm obviously giving off."

He chuckled. "You have a vivid imagination. Fine, let's see... I guess my most pressing deal right now is a mall project."

"A mall, huh?"

"Yeah. But it's in a small town, and we've got a noisy environmental group trying to stop it."

"Oh. Will they be able to?"

"Nah, I highly doubt it. We have more than enough money to fight it until we bankrupt them."

Her eyebrows furrowed. "You would do that? Try to bankrupt a group that's just trying to protect the town they love?"

He eyed her carefully. "I wouldn't do it on purpose, no. But this is business, and a lot of money and time has been invested in this. We don't go down without a fight."

She almost looked irritated. "But a mall? I mean, is that worth fighting for? There are malls all over the country, right?"

"Do you just enjoy arguing?"

She smiled. "Sorry. I was on the debate team in high school." Lies, all lies.

"Well, I bet you got an A in that class."

Daisy was fuming inside. Bankrupt the group? What kind of man was he? Every time she thought he might be a decent, nice guy, he showed his true colors. She couldn't imagine everything in life being about money.

And then she'd lied and said she was on the debate team in high school. Her school didn't even have a debate team. They didn't even have a cafeteria. They'd had to drag out tables into the gym to eat lunch everyday.

"So, I take it you don't like malls?"

"Not really. I'm more of a thrift store kind of gal," she said without thinking. His eyebrows knitted together. "I mean, I like bringing vintage items back from the brink."

"Interesting. I don't think I've ever been in a thrift store."

"Really? I'll have to take you to one some time," she said. Take him to one? Like they were going to be lifelong buddies and go on adventures together?

Tristan didn't say anything else about the mall or their thrift store plans. He probably thought she was an idiot at this point. After all, who was in their late twenties and was scared of the beach? Of course, he was scared of clowns, and they were just fun birthday party characters as far as she was concerned. At least her fear made sense.

Without warning, another boat zipped past them going very fast and sending a wave in their direction. As Santa yelled at them, shaking his fist in the air, the boat lurched upward, sending Daisy into a panic. She tensed up and instinctively reached for Tristan's hands, holding onto them for dear life.

Tristan glanced at his daughter, made sure she was still okay, and then stared down at their inter-locked fingers.

"It's okay, Daisy. We're fine. It was just a rogue wave." His voice was soothing as he watched her hyperventilating. Still, she couldn't let go of his hands. It was like they were glued together, and as dumb as she felt, she just couldn't let go.

Finally, the boat felt level again, and she slowly loosened her grip. Embarrassment overtook her, and she put her face in her hands.

"Oh my gosh, I'm so sorry. Did I hurt you?"

Tristan laughed. "I'm tougher than I look. You okay?"

He actually looked concerned. No, no, no. She wasn't falling for the nice guy act again. This was the guy talking about bankrupting her environmental group and building a mall in her town.

"What's that?" Daisy asked as she caught a glance of something in the water on their side of the boat. "Is that a shark?"

Tristan turned at the same time Santa did.

"Lookie there, folks! We've got us a dolphin over here!"

All of the kids ran to their side and giggled with delight as they watched the dolphin breaking through the water over and over again, following them as they moved. Daisy had to admit it was invigorating to see the beautiful creature chasing them. For a moment, the ocean wasn't as scary as it had been a few moments before.

After the dolphin disappeared back to the depths, the kids ran back to the other side, leaving Tristan and Daisy alone again.

"You know, if you get scared again, you're

welcome to hold my hand," he said, in what was the most unexpected thing anyone had ever said to her.

~

What was he doing? Asking Elliana's nanny to hold his hand? He needed a girlfriend and quick. Obviously, he was lacking female attention or something. After all, he and Daisy couldn't be more different if they tried. He just kept replaying that moment over and over again as they made their way back to the house for dinner.

He remembered his grandfather saying something when he was a kid. Everyone always pointed out how different his grandfather had been from his grandmother. After all, he was a hardened cop and his grandmother had been a prim and proper violin teacher. Grandpa had said, "If you're both the same, one of you's unnecessary."

But Tristan seemed to always attract the same type of woman - stuffy, overly made up, addicted to shopping and using his money to do it. There was never much below the surface. The only woman he'd ever had true feelings for was Elliana's mother, but even that union wasn't made in heaven. They got along well, until they didn't. But Elliana had come from love, even if it was short lived.

Still, he wondered briefly what his circle of rich friends would have to say about him dating his daughter's nanny. Surely, the gossip mill would run full steam on that one for months.

"How do you like your steak?" he asked as he stood at the grill, the ocean waves lapping the shore behind the deck. The sun was getting ready to set, and Elliana had requested dinner as a family. Right now, Daisy was part of that family.

"Well done, please."

"Seriously? You know that turns this beautiful piece of meat into shoe leather, right?"

She smiled and shrugged her shoulders. "You asked, I answered."

"Terrible. Absolutely terrible," he muttered as he looked back down. "I like mine to be rare enough that a good veterinarian could possibly resuscitate it."

Daisy let out a loud laugh that surprised him. He turned to see her trying not to spit her soda everywhere. Tristan handed her a napkin.

"Sorry. I don't know why that was so funny to me." She wiped her mouth and a stray drop from her shirt.

"I'm a funny guy, what can I say?"

"And humble too," she retorted.

"When are we eating? I'm starving!" Elliana asked as she twirled around on the deck.

"Well, your chicken fingers are almost done in the oven. Why don't you go check the timer for me?" Tristan said. Elliana ran into the house.

"Listen, thanks for not blowing my cover today about being scared of the ocean. I don't want Elliana to think I'm a big loser," Daisy whispered.

Tristan turned and looked at her. She was a pretty woman, for sure. Not at all the type he normally attracted, though. She wore little makeup, just a hint of pink lip gloss. Her hair was natural and didn't even seem to be dyed or highlighted. It was a cross between dirty blond and brown with hints of auburn.

"Hello?" she said, waving her hand in front of his face.

Tristan froze for a moment. How long had he been staring at her looking like an idiot? Right now, it felt like hours.

"Sorry. I was trying to remember if I put the baked potatoes in the oven."

"You did. Want me to check the timer on that too?"

"Nah. They've still got a bit of time left. And don't worry about looking like a loser. Elliana thinks you hung the moon."

"Really? You think so?"

He smiled. "She loved her old nanny. Tatiana was like a mother to her. But in the short time you've been here, I can definitely see her warming up to you. I just hate that..."

"That what?"

"Well, I don't like to see her get attached to people who won't be around long."

Daisy's face fell in a way he didn't expect. Surely she had a life to go back to? Did she think there was a chance she was getting a longterm job with him? He decided not to ask. He found it was better to change the subject in situations like this.

"Anyway, got any plans for you two this week?"

Daisy cleared her throat, obviously understanding that they were moving on to another topic. "I was thinking about taking her to Savannah, if you don't mind us borrowing the car one day?"

"Savannah?"

"Yes. It's not too far, and I'd love to take her to the children's museum there."

"That sounds good. I like for her to get educational opportunities during the summer as much as possible."

"Good. I'll look into it further and let you know what day."

He smiled slightly. "Thanks."

"I hope you know you can trust me, Mr. Spencer."

He paused for a moment, studying her expression. "Please call me Tristan, Miss Davenport."

"Only if you call me Daisy."

CHAPTER 7

*D*aisy stood in the powder room, staring at her reflection. She leaned over and splashed more cold water on her face and then studied herself in the mirror again.

What had she gotten herself into? This was feeling more and more dangerous by the second.

The danger of Tristan learning who she was and why she was really there.

The danger of getting attached to Elliana and breaking the little girl's heart in the process.

The danger of staring too hard at Tristan's smoldering good looks and catching herself on fire in the process.

Their dolphin cruise had been both terrifying and invigorating in the process. Although the dolphins were cute, she found herself sneaking glances at the man holding her hands more often than she should have.

This was bad. All of it. There was no upside. So far, she'd found absolutely no way to talk him out of the mall project, and she had no real plan on how she would ever accomplish what she came there to do.

She was stuck. She could pack her things and sneak out under cover of darkness, but what would that accomplish? At least she was getting paid for her work. And Elliana was a good kid.

But she had to at least try to stop the project because at the end of the summer, she had to go home. Back to Thornhill. And she didn't want a big, ugly mall in her backyard.

She had to find a way, no matter how handsome her target was.

"Are you coming out of there?" Elliana called from the other side of the door. Embarrassed, Daisy opened the door and smiled at the little girl. "Why is your face so red?"

"Elliana! Don't be so nosy," Tristan said, pulling his daughter by her shoulders into the kitchen. "Sorry," he mouthed as they walked away.

Daisy followed them into the kitchen, hoping Tristan wasn't wondering why her face was so red too. She quickly busied herself getting the food and carried it to the table.

Dinner was easier than she'd thought it would be, their conversation flowing freely. Tristan talked about his upbringing in Virginia, as well as losing both of his parents when he was in college. First, his mother had died of cancer, and then his father died of a heart attack months later.

"I believe in broken heart syndrome," he said, almost under his breath.

"Your father, you mean?"

"Yes. I watched him sink further and further into depression after my mother died. There was nothing I could do for him. He just couldn't be on this Earth without her, I guess."

Elliana excused herself to go to the restroom, leaving the two of them alone to continue talking. They walked out onto the deck while they waited for the ice cream dessert cake they'd bought to thaw on the counter.

"I've always envied people who get to experience that kind of love," Daisy said without thinking. She leaned on her forearms against the deck, looking out over the now darkened ocean.

Tristan, who was leaning beside her, chuckled softly. "Me too. My parents had one of those love affairs that you see in cheesy chick flicks."

"Not a fan of chick flicks, huh?" Daisy asked, desperately trying to change the subject from falling in love.

He smiled. "Not really. What about you? Do you like those kinds of movies?"

Daisy shook her head. "Call me jaded, but I

think the way love is portrayed in movies is pure crap."

Tristan laughed. "Well, tell me how you really feel!"

She suddenly felt really stupid. Who talks to their boss that way?

"Sorry. I can be a bit blunt when I'm not thinking."

He turned toward her, one elbow resting on the deck rail. "I like that in a person. No need to mince words, right?"

"Right." The less words she said, the better.

"So, where did you grow up?"

The question made her freeze in place. She couldn't say Thornhill, but if she said another area and he had questions she couldn't answer...

"Sorry, that was a personal question. You don't have to answer that."

Before Daisy could come up with something to say, Elliana came bounding outside. It was like the kid was on speed all the time.

"Let's play a game!" she said, a stack of board games in her arms obscuring her face. Tristan grabbed the stack from her and looked at Daisy.

"Are you game?" he said, proud of his pun-making ability.

She nodded and followed them back into the house. They spread the games out and decided to start with Scrabble, even though Elliana wasn't the best at spelling just yet. Tristan said he wanted to challenge her.

For hours, they ate cake and played games and laughed more than Daisy had expected. He didn't seem like her boss tonight, but more like a friend. Or more than a friend.

No. She couldn't allow herself to have those feelings. More and more, she had to remind herself of the original intention of this whole thing. To save her town, and herself, from the blight of a shopping mall. This summer would be over soon, and he'd be gone, back to his snazzy life in the city. She wasn't going to be left looking at busty blonds with shopping bags in her backyard.

"Elliana, it's time for bed. Run up and get ready. I'll come read you a story and tuck you in."

She quickly hugged Daisy goodnight and ran up the stairs, still with more energy than one human should have. As Daisy cleaned up, Tristan went up and got his daughter in bed. Awhile later, he joined her on the deck, a bottle of wine and two glasses in his hands.

"Care for a glass?"

Daisy nodded. "Sure. Maybe just one." Daisy wasn't much of a drinker, especially after losing her mother to addiction.

They sat in silence for a few moments, enjoying the wine and the sound of the waves. It was strange that the sounds of the ocean wasn't scaring her as much now. She still had no plans to scuba dive or go deep sea fishing, but now she could enjoy the beauty and peaceful sounds, at least.

"I think Elliana had a good time today. Don't you?" he asked, almost like he was looking for reassurance.

"Absolutely. She was all smiles today."

"It's hard because I don't always get this kind of time with her. My business can be a bit... demanding."

Taking her opportunity, Daisy spoke. "Maybe you need to cut down on the number of deals you're involved in?"

He cocked his head at her, one eyebrow raised. She'd obviously said the wrong thing.

"Pardon?"

"Well, I just mean... well, you're a billionaire, right? I mean, do you have to work so much?"

She was getting in too deep, but for some reason she couldn't shut off her big mouth.

"And how do you think I got to where I am? By cutting back on my business? I do everything for my daughter, Daisy."

"Do you?"

"Wow. I don't even know what to say." He sat back in his chair a bit, and she could see his jaw twitching in the moonlight.

"I'm sorry. I didn't mean to offend you. I just

thought that maybe if there was a deal you could let go, it would free up more time..."

He looked at her, his gaze now impassable. "Excuse me for saying so, but I don't take business advice from a nanny. Goodnight, Miss Davenport."

Without another word, he stood, walked inside and went straight up the stairs. Daisy was both embarrassed and angry. So a nanny was beneath him? What kind of guy said something like that? And now she was Miss Davenport again?

Any qualms she'd had about thwarting his business plans for her town were now gone. She'd stop this project if it was the last thing she did.

Tristan sat on the edge of his bed, his fists clenched. What right did she have to say those things? And why was it bothering him so much?

If he really searched his heart, it was because she was right. He hadn't spent enough time with his daughter, and he knew that. But listening to someone else point it out just hit way too close to home.

Another part of him realized it was because he was developing feelings for this woman. Feelings he shouldn't have. There was no future here. They were from two vastly different worlds, and the summer would be over in a few weeks. Each of them would go back to their worlds, him to his rich and wealthy lifestyle and her back to... Well, wherever she came from.

This was temporary. He just kept repeating that phrase in his mind over and over. He knew he was doing what he always did - getting angry at a woman so as not to develop feelings for her. Feelings were a very dangerous thing. It was much better to date women he didn't really have an emotional attraction to. It saved his sanity, his bank account and his little daughter's heart.

He stood up and walked over to the mirror, staring at his reflection. Who had he become? He hadn't grown up super wealthy. He'd built his company from the ground up. Was he becoming one of those people who thought other people were beneath him? That was the last thing he wanted to model for his daughter.

But it wasn't because he thought Daisy was beneath him, was it? No. It wasn't that. It was because she would be gone soon and he didn't want to get himself into a sticky situation with a woman who wasn't staying.

And even if she was staying, even if he offered her a long-term job, what kind of man dated his daughter's nanny? What kind of publicity would that get him?

And what did he really know about her, anyway?

He didn't know where she was from, anything about her family, what her future plans were... All he knew was that she was scared of the ocean, was a wicked Scrabble player and was incredibly adorable.

No. Not adorable. Stop saying adorable, he thought to himself.

He decided he would just think of her as "temporarily adorable".

Ugh. Life was way too complicated.

D aisy tossed and turned in her bed. It had been two hours since she laid her head on the pillow, but she was finding herself growing more and more irritated at her wealthy boss two rooms down. Sleep was elusive tonight.

She kept running through options in her mind, ways that she could derail his plans. But the truth was, she was no businesswoman. She didn't have any clue how to stop this from happening. She decided she would call Megan the next day and see if she could bounce some ideas around.

There was a part of her that had enjoyed the evening. She felt herself strangely drawn to this man, although he was completely out of her league financially. She thought about all of the money he had in his bank account. What in the world would a person do with all of that money? She wondered whether he was doing anything good with it or hoarding it all for himself when there were so many needy people in the world.

She decided that he was hoarding it just so she could get angrier at him.

But the angrier she got, the more she thought about how handsome he was. The dimple. The pearly white teeth that didn't look fake. The crystal clear blue eyes that looked like the ocean and probably scared her a little bit more. The stubble that formed every evening around his jaw line, the one she found herself struggling not to stare at over dinner.

Thankfully, he was probably busy every day for the rest of the summer. After all, this was just an anomaly. It was one day that his guilty conscience overtook him and made him spend it with his daughter.

Most likely, she'd have the rest of the summer to lay around by the pool, watch Elliana play on the beach and even read a good book every now and again.

Just as she was starting to drift off, she heard something from the other room. At first, she didn't think much of it but then the sound persisted. She decided to get up and make sure that Elliana was okay. She slipped on her robe, opened her door and crept across the hallway as quietly as she could. The last thing she wanted to do was have another interaction with Tristan tonight.

When she opened Elliana's door, the little girl was covered up to her neck, as if she was freezing. It was warm outside, so Daisy immediately knew something was wrong.

"Elliana, what's going on?

"I don't know. I woke up feeling kind of bad and my teeth are chattering."

Daisy could see her shaking and, with the moonlight streaming through the window, she could see sweat forming across her brow.

"I think you have a fever," she said, touching her forehead. There was no thinking about it. She definitely had a fever, and a high one.

"I don't feel so good. It feels kind of like my breathing is bad."

Daisy immediately became frightened. Asthma was nothing to mess around with, especially with a high fever.

"Wait here. I'm going to get your dad." She ran out of the room and over to Tristan's door. It was shut, so she opened it without thinking. She found him standing there wearing nothing but a pair of boxer briefs.

"What are you doing in here?" he asked, quickly reaching for the robe draped over the end of his bed.

Daisy turned her eyes away. "Sorry. I wasn't thinking. Elliana is sick..."

Before she could say anything else, he ran past her and straight into his daughter's room.

"Eliana, what's wrong, sweetie?"

Over the next few minutes, Elliana gave him the same information. They found a thermometer in the bathroom drawer and took her temperature. It was 102°.

"Should I call the pediatrician here in town?" Daisy asked.

"No. I think we should take her to the emergency room."

CHAPTER 8

The ride to the emergency room had been quiet, with each of them paying close attention to any noises coming from Elliana in the backseat. Daisy found herself more worried than she thought she'd be about someone else's child. But she was growing close to the little girl, and she was definitely concerned.

Or maybe they were quiet because of the way they'd left things. She didn't know for sure, and now certainly wasn't the time to try to figure it out.

They pulled into the hospital parking lot, and Tristan parked the car as close to the building as possible. They both jumped out quickly, opening Elliana's door. In one swift motion, he reached inside and grabbed his little girl in his arms, walking quickly toward the sliding doors to the emergency room.

There was something about the way that he

moved, the way that he took charge, that made Daisy see a different side of him. He was probably this way in business, making quick decisions and showing authority.

But this was a different kind of strength. This was a father doing whatever he had to for his daughter. She could feel the fear around him as he walked up to the desk and immediately started talking before the woman even had a chance to ask him what was wrong.

"My daughter is sick. She has a high fever and asthma. She needs to see someone now."

"Sir, if you'll just write her name here on the sign in sheet, we'll call you back in just a moment..."

Tristan stared at the woman. "No. She's very ill, and she needs to see someone right now."

"Tristan..." Daisy tried to say, touching his arm.

He glared at her before looking back at the woman. "My name is Tristan Spencer. I could buy this hospital right now. Do you understand me?"

Daisy was taken aback. His voice was deeper and gruffer than she'd ever heard it. This was a father who was terrified. The woman behind the desk just stood there for a moment, obviously dumbfounded.

"Tristan? Let me hold Elliana over here in the chair, okay? I'm sure they have some legal forms you need to fill out."

He stood there for a moment and then looked at Daisy, regret on his face. He took a breath and then carefully handed his daughter over to Daisy. Elliana was big for her age, and Daisy was small for hers, so she quickly made her way to the waiting area and sat down with Elliana cradled in her lap.

Tristan watched as they got settled into a chair and then looked back at the woman. Daisy couldn't hear what he said, but the look on his face was apologetic, and the woman was smiling sadly and nodding.

Within minutes, they were ushered to the back. Elliana was awake but not overly alert. She was very weak which was a far cry from how she'd been the entire day between the dolphin cruise and playing games. She had seemed perfectly fine.

Nurses descended upon her quickly, changing her into a gown and taking her vital signs. Daisy watched as they looked at each other, obvious concern on their faces.

January Cove was a small town, and the hospital was definitely not state of the art. She wondered if there was something more dangerous going on that they couldn't handle there. Where would they send her? She knew that Tristan would do whatever was necessary for his daughter.

"She's going to be okay," Daisy finally said. Of course, she had no way of knowing that, but she wanted to say something, anything, to try to ease Tristan's mind. He leaned over in his chair, forearms on his knees, staring at his sleeping daughter.

"I hope you're right. I just don't understand this. She seemed fine all day, even at bedtime."

"I've heard that kids can get really sick, really fast, but the good thing is they usually bounce back quickly."

She didn't know what she was talking about, having never been around kids herself. All she could do was regurgitate information she'd heard other people say over the years.

"Have any of the kids you've been a nanny for gotten sick like this?" It was an obvious question that she hadn't seen coming, for some reason. He looked tired and worried, and she felt horribly guilty for the lie that was about the come out of her mouth.

"Of course. All the time."

All the time? What in the world was that supposed to mean?

"Really?" Now, he really looked concerned. He probably thought she did something to cause this.

"Well, I mean, kids get all kinds of viruses and so forth... You know, I bet it was one of those kids on the dolphin cruise." Better to pass the buck.

"I'm not sure she could've gotten so sick that quickly..."

"Let's just wait for the doctor," Daisy said, trying to sound reassuring but really just wanting to take the focus off of her stupid comments.

They waited for what seemed like an eternity, with Elliana waking up and falling asleep over and over. She groaned in her sleep, and Tristan would console her as best he could. The look of desperation on his face made Daisy feel sorry for him.

Nurses also came in and out, taking vitals and blood. They even did a chest X-ray using a portable machine. The waiting was the hardest part.

"I feel bad about how I acted out there earlier," he said. "I'm not the kind of guy who tries to use his position to get better treatment. Or at least I didn't think I was." He stared at his daughter, his eyes tired.

Early morning sunlight peeked through the window blinds. "I understand. In situations like this, we use whatever we have to to help those we love."

He touched Elliana's little hand. "She's my world."

Daisy sat further up in her chair. "She'll be okay. I just know it."

Tristan looked at her, an appreciative look on his face. It was almost like he wanted to say something, but the doctor walked into the room.

"Are you Elliana's father?"

"Yes, I am."

"I'm Dr. James," he said. He was a younger, handsome man, which Daisy hadn't expected given the age of the hospital. "I'd like to talk to you about what's going on with your daughter."

"Okay."

"Elliana is suffering from the flu."

"But she had her shot..."

"Unfortunately, the shot doesn't cover every strain. If it was just the flu we were dealing with, I'd send you home with instructions to give her fluids and make her comfortable."

"But that's not all?" Tristan asked, standing up.

"No. I wish it was. Elliana has developed pneumonia in one of her lungs, and that has triggered her asthma. We're also a little concerned about some of her lab work."

"Concerned?"

"We always want to be aware of the possibility of a bacterial infection so we can treat it immediately. I'm sure you've heard of sepsis?"

"Oh my gosh..." Tristan said, hanging onto the side of Elliana's bed. Daisy stood beside him and placed her hand over his.

"Will she be okay?" Daisy asked, giving Tristan time to take in what the doctor was saying.

"We'd like to admit her for the time being so we can give her IV antibiotics and fluids. We should know more within twenty-four hours."

The doctor's non-answer made Daisy feel scared, but she didn't want Tristan to know that. This was serious.

After the doctor left the room, Daisy sat back down, but Tristan leaned over his daughter, rubbing his thumb on her cheek as she slept.

"You were right."

"Right? About what?"

"I wasn't making enough time for her. This is my fault."

Daisy stood up again and touched his arm, something she was getting way too used to doing. His arms were nice, especially when they were uncovered instead of being forced inside of a dress shirt.

"This is not your fault, Tristan. Kids catch things all the time. We got her here early, and I know they're going to do everything to..."

He turned around swiftly. "To what? Save her life? Do you think this is life threatening?"

The look on his face wasn't that of a big, strong billionaire. It was almost like he was a scared, young boy looking for reassurance. Daisy thought about how long he'd been at this parenting thing alone. It was different for a woman to raise a child alone. After all, most women had that innate mothering instinct. But, for a man, it had to be harder. Male instincts were just different to her, somehow.

In that moment, it made more sense to her that he'd opted for work rather than spending more time with Elliana. He wanted to protect her, but in a much more "male" way than she needed. He was looking at her future financial protection, and not realizing she needed more emotional protection as a young girl learning her way in the world.

"No. That's not what I meant at all. I just know they'll do everything they can to get her better so we can have the next few weeks to enjoy January Cove. She's going to be great, Tristan."

She stared into his blue eyes and realized she could easily get lost in them. He looked like he needed her in that moment, and she really needed to be needed by someone. Especially a hot billionaire. Who didn't want to be needed by one of those?

"Maybe I should move her to Atlanta? That way I'd be closer to my house, and we'd have the best of doctors."

Daisy shrugged her shoulders. "Or maybe she'll get more personalized care in a place like this?"

"It's possible. Still, I think I'm going to make some calls. See if my doctor friends can make recommendations down here. Maybe we can get a specialist over from Savannah or something. Do you mind sitting with her for a little bit? I'll just be right outside the door."

"Take all the time you need."

Tristan walked out, and Daisy turned back to Elliana's bedside. Did she know how much her daddy loved her? How much he agonized over every decision he made as it related to her?

And what would he think if he realized the woman he just left standing in the room with her was a complete fraud and not even the nanny he hired? The guilt made her queasy sometimes. She felt like an animal with its leg caught in a trap. No matter what she did, she was in a bad situation.

She looked at Elliana's sweet face and thought about how everything could go bad so quickly, and how there were many more important things in the world than a stupid mall. The little girl's health was on the line. Suddenly, that was all that really mattered to her.

Tristan made call after call from the hallway, poking his head in to check on Elliana a few times. The last time, Daisy was fast asleep in the chair next to her, holding his daughter's hand in hers.

He was terrified. Absolutely more scared than he'd ever been in his life. The biggest financial risks he'd taken, even early in his career, didn't come close to giving him the type of fear he had right now.

His daughter had to live.

He knew how bad this was. His own aunt had died of sepsis in the hospital after a surgery on her hip. He never wanted to hear that word again, especially not as it related to his own child.

Guilt wracked his body as he thought about all the missed time with her. There were so many times she wanted him to read her a second book or watch a silly movie with her, and he'd made excuses and had Tatiana do those things with her.

What must his daughter think of him inside her

small, precious little brain? Was she disappointed in him? Did she wish she had a different father who would spend more time with her? Did she know how much he loved her?

The only thing keeping him remotely calm was Daisy. They'd gone to bed so angry at each other, yet she'd remained his rock through the whole ordeal. If he had to do this alone... well, he couldn't have.

After making multiple calls to friends in the medical industry back in Atlanta, Tristan finally felt confident enough to stay in January Cove. Most of them said the hospital should be completely adept at handling this sort of situation, but one of his friends recommended a pediatrician in Savannah that might be willing to travel to the hospital to do a consultation. Tristan had found, given his immense financial assets, pretty much anyone would do anything for the right amount. And he was willing to spare no expense when it came to his daughter.

He walked back into the room to find Daisy asleep in the chair, still holding his daughter's hand. He looked at her and wondered who she really was. Where had she really come from? Why was she so reluctant to talk about her past?

But more importantly, why hadn't some lucky guy snatched her up already?

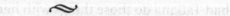

Daisy was embarrassed when she woke up to find Tristan staring at her from the next chair. She had fallen asleep holding Eliana's hand, and to be honest, she had completely lost track of time.

"Sorry. What time is it?"

"Don't worry. You didn't miss lunch. But the nurse did come in a few minutes ago and say that we are moving to the new room shortly."

"Oh good. I know you'll be glad to have Elliana in her own room so that she can start getting the care she needs." Daisy stood up to stretch, carefully letting go of Elliana's hand. The little girl stirred and opened her eyes.

"Where am I?" she asked.

Tristan immediately stood up and walked over, leaning down over his daughter and smiling.

"We brought you to see the doctor, sweetie. Remember, you weren't feeling well last night?"

"I feel really bad. When can we go home?"

Tristan looked back at Daisy.

"They are going to put you in your own room for a little while, just to give you the right medicine. Then we will be able to go back to the beach house and enjoy the rest of our summer. Does that sound good?"

She nodded sleepily and then closed her eyes again. Tristan stood there for a few moments, squeezing her tiny hand in his. After a few minutes, they could hear her light snoring begin again.

"This is the hardest thing I've ever gone through, and we've only been here a few hours."

Daisy sat down in the chair. "I don't know how parents do this for months on end. I had a friend whose little boy had pediatric cancer, and they were in the hospital for months at a time. I don't think I'd be strong enough for something like that."

Tristan nodded his head. "I'm not even sure I'm strong enough for something like *this*."

Daisy smiled. It was kind of nice seeing this side of him that wasn't so sure of himself, although she would've preferred to have seen that in just about any other situation than his child being sick.

"Look, these doctors know what they're doing. They deal with this kind of thing every day. I just know that she's in good hands."

"Well, just in case, I have one of the top pediatric specialists coming in from Savannah later today. Hopefully he will be able to shed some light on her situation and make sure that we're making the proper treatment decisions."

Daisy nodded. "Do you mind if I step out and stretch my legs a little bit before they move us?"

"Of course not. Listen, I know this isn't your responsibility. I mean, you're not a nurse or anything. If you'd rather go back to the beach house and wait there..."

She shook her head. "No. I'd much rather stay here with you guys. I would just be worried sitting there anyway."

Tristan cocked his head slightly, a quirk of a smile on his face. "Okay then. I'll see you when you come back."

She stood there for a moment longer than necessary, both of them looking at each other. It was like he was surprised that she wanted to stay with Elliana, but wasn't that what she had been hired for? To make sure that the little girl was okay?

She stepped out and walked out into the courtyard just off the parking lot. She stretched her legs and leaned over to stretch her back before digging her cell phone out of her pocket.

"Hello?"

"Meg, thank goodness you answered. You're not going to believe what happened."

For the next few minutes, she explained everything that had happened from the dolphin cruise up to the present moment.

"I hope she's going to be alright. It sounds kind of serious."

"I'm worried that it is. Of course, I'm trying to tell Tristan that everything's going to be fine, but I'm not really sure myself. Just say a prayer for her," Daisy said.

"Of course. So what about your plan?"

Daisy paused for a moment. "I don't know. It feels

terrible to even talk about something like that right now. I have the rest of the summer to worry about it. Right now, I just want to focus on getting her better. I feel guilty enough about all of this as it is. I never should've done this."

"I tried to tell you..."

"Really? Now is not the time to do the 'I told you so' thing!"

Megan sighed. "You're right. I'm sorry. I'll be thinking about you, and please at least send me a text to update me after you meet with the specialist."

"I will. And don't forget to pray for her."

By the time Daisy got back to the room, the nurse was already there to move Elliana. They didn't even wake her up. Instead, they just slowly slid her from one bed to another and rolled her up to her room. The hospital was fairly small, but it still had three stories. Eliana was on the second floor with a room overlooking the ocean across the main road.

Once they got settled in, Tristan turned on the TV as a distraction. The room wasn't all that big and only had one place to sit which was a long, built-in sofa. They took turns sitting on the end of Elliana's bed or sitting on the sofa, as if they couldn't sit so close on that little sofa.

"Anything in particular you want to watch?" Tristan asked once all of the news programs were over for the evening.

"Not really. I'm not much of a TV person. I much prefer watching movies."

"I'm not sure I could even concentrate on a movie right now, to be honest," he said.

"I don't think I could either."

They sat there in silence, the TV on mute, for quite a long time. The nurse came in to update Elliana's vitals and check her IV. They had started some high-dose antibiotics for her pneumonia and were also giving her fluids for the flu.

"I'm starving. What about you?"

"I could eat," Daisy said. "Do you want me to run down to the cafeteria..."

Tristan let out a chuckle. "I don't think the cafeteria is what I'm looking for. There's got to be somewhere around here with good food."

"How about I take the car and do a little sleuthing around. I'm sure I can find something we can enjoy."

"Okay. Here, take my card. And here are the keys to the car. Just get whatever you think we might need for the foreseeable future. Oh, and Elliana loves those little apple juice boxes. Maybe get some of those. You know, just in case she can have something tomorrow."

Daisy smiled. "I'm sure she's going to want those very soon. I'll be back as quickly as I can."

He nodded appreciatively. Her heart did a little jump that she wasn't expecting. They were starting to feel like some kind of couple, sitting at the hospital together battling against an illness that was affecting the child they both cared about. Man, she had really gotten herself into a pickle.

CHAPTER 9

By the time Daisy got back with dinner, Elliana had woken up for a little while. She was still very weak, but the nurse was encouraged that she seemed to be improving slightly. Still, they were worried about her getting a bacterial infection in her blood and wanted to keep her for at least a couple of days.

She was awake long enough to do a breathing treatment, but fell asleep not long after. Daisy thought that was very telling about how tired the little girl was since breathing treatments usually made her hyper, Tristan said. But she went right to sleep, her poor little body trying to fight off whatever was attacking it.

"You haven't touched your sandwich. I thought you were hungry?"

Tristan stood and stared out the large glass window. The sun had gone down, and moonlight was all that could be seen over the ocean water across the street. The little town was not exactly a hotbed of activity, so there were no skyscrapers or lights to see off in the distance. Instead, there was only the occasional light in one of the oceanfront cottages or the flicker of a light on a passing boat.

"I guess I lost my appetite. Seeing her struggle like that, with her breathing, it always scares me. No matter how many times I've seen her have an asthma attack, it never gets any easier."

Daisy stood up. She stared out at the blackness of the ocean. "I don't have children, so I can't say that I totally understand. But you're doing a great job. Being a single parent has to be one of the most difficult things anyone can ever do."

He shrugged his shoulders. "You know, she had a great mother. I mean, we weren't together when she died, obviously, but we always stayed friendly for the sake of Elliana. I just hope that I make the right decisions for her. A little girl needs a mother, and I'm just not sure I'm doing both jobs very well."

"Don't say that. You're doing great."

He turned and faced her. "I don't think you mean that. Wasn't it you who just told me I wasn't spending enough time with my daughter?"

Her stomach churned. "Look, I wasn't trying to say anything negative. I was just pointing out how excited she seemed to get to spend some time with you."

He sighed before sitting down in the chair again. "I guess I find it kind of hard to balance everything. Even with a nanny, I have this guilt in the back of my mind all the time that I'm not doing enough for her. I want her future to be set in stone. I don't want her to ever have to struggle or worry about paying her bills or stay in a bad situation with some guy financially supporting her."

Daisy sat down and smiled. "See? That's what a good dad does. He thinks far ahead and tries to slay those dragons before they even rear their ugly faces."

He leaned forward and squeezed Elliana's little hand as it hung off the bed. "I guess. That's why I wish she still had her mother around. Somebody to comfort her and cuddle with her and answer all of those questions that I know are coming soon. What do I know about bras and makeup and the feminine aisle at the grocery store? I mean, I'm not exactly her go-to person for those kinds of questions. Honestly, raising a daughter alone is a lot scarier than running a billion dollar business."

She couldn't believe he was opening up like this. It was a whole different side of him. It was also unbelievably attractive.

Maybe if she just told him the truth right now, that she was there to thwart his mall deal, he would understand. He was obviously a lot more sensitive than she had given him credit for.

"So how will you handle your business while

Elliana is sick? I mean, is there somebody who can take over for you?"

"I have an assistant, but he can't make the big decisions. I'm sure he'll be texting me updates about a deal we're working on."

"What kind of deal?" she asked, nonchalantly.

"It's that mall that we're building in a small town. There's a little group of people that are getting louder and louder in opposition. I really don't understand it."

Now was her chance. Find out exactly what he was thinking about this deal and why it was so important to him.

"Why are they upset?"

"I'm not really sure. I think, you know, it's just a little country town and they are used to things staying the same. But things can't always stay the same. You have to have progress, and that's what I'm trying to do for this town. They'll make money, I'll make money, hundreds of jobs will be provided. As far as I can tell, it's a win/win situation."

"Well, maybe progress isn't always necessary. I mean, if every place in the world had development, we wouldn't have the Eiffel Tower or the Sphinx. There'd be some strip mall there with pawn shops and check-cashing places."

Tristan laughed. "I think that might be a little bit dramatic. But I get your point."

Before she could get more in depth in the

conversation, the doctor came in to give an update. Everything was pretty much the same, but they were happy with Elliana's progress and that she was stable at the moment. They also told Tristan that the specialist should be arriving soon, and they wanted him to meet with Tristan in another room so that Elliana couldn't hear their discussion.

Tristan agreed. He didn't want Elliana to worry any more than she needed to. And who knew what the little girl could possibly hear or understand while they were discussing things in her room.

"I'll stay here with her, just in case she wakes up. You go ahead."

Tristan followed the doctor out of the room to go meet with the specialist. Daisy assumed they would come back with the new doctor and allow him to assess Elliana at some point. But for now, she had the quiet, darkened room to enjoy all to herself.

She leaned back on the sofa and tried to relax. She hadn't gotten any sleep in so many hours, and she was pretty exhausted. Just as she was dozing off, she felt a vibration. She shifted her weight only to realize that Tristan's phone was under her shoulder. It must've fallen out of his pocket.

She knew she shouldn't have done it. She tried to keep herself from looking, but the thought of his assistant sending him a message about the mall project was just too enticing.

When she looked down, she saw someone's

name and a text that said "The mall deal is up in the air. They've had a better offer from the Dempsey Corporation out in California. Something about saving the land for conservation. These stupid environmental groups are such a pain! They are giving you a deadline of tonight at midnight to sign off on the final paperwork without changes. If you don't sign, the other contract from Dempsey will automatically be accepted. Let me know what to do, boss."

Daisy sat there, her hand shaking as she kept checking the door. What should she do? If she deleted the text, there was a good chance that he would lose the deal and never know she had anything to do with it. Just a text lost in the digital cloud everyone was always talking about.

She looked over and checked that Elliana was still fast asleep, and she was. The light snoring from her bed was a constant sound in the room, like some kind of ambient noise machine.

She quickly dialed Megan's number and stood in the corner of the room. Hopefully, Tristan wouldn't walk in and wonder why she was chatting with a friend in his daughter's hospital room, but she couldn't leave the little girl there alone.

"Megan? Can you hear me?" she asked, whispering softly into the phone. She turned herself so that she could see the door in case Tristan and the doctors came back.

"Yeah. What's going on? Did something happen to Elliana?"

"No, she's about the same. Tristan is meeting with the specialist now. But listen, I need some advice. I have an opportunity to stop this deal, but I feel so guilty doing it while Elliana is in the hospital. I need you to talk me down off the ledge."

"Oh goodness. What's happening?"

"He left his phone in here. I think it must've fallen out of his pocket. Anyway, he has this message from his assistant saying they have until midnight tonight to finalize this deal. If he doesn't hear from him, it's going to someone else and the whole thing will be over. They will make it conservation land from some environmental company out in California. That's the best case scenario. If I just delete this text..."

"Are you kidding? Are you really thinking about doing that while his daughter is in the hospital?"

"I know it makes me a terrible person, but I might not get another chance like this. I don't think I'm hurting anyone. I'm still here for Elliana, I'm still helping him. He's a billionaire. He's never going to miss the money, but my town will never be the same if they build this stupid mall there. All I have to do is hit delete and this whole thing will be over. Then I can just enjoy the rest of the summer doing my job."

"The fact that you're calling me and asking my opinion means that you don't feel sure about what you're doing. This is a big deal, Daisy. You're ruining part of his business. I'm not sure that's the right thing for you to be doing..."

"Why did I call you? You always have to try to be the voice of reason. Oh crap, I hear them coming. I have to go."

She quickly ended her phone call as she heard Tristan and the doctors' voices just outside of the door. She had to make a decision right now. Quick thinking had never worked to her benefit, and this was probably going to end up biting her in the butt before it was over with.

She looked down and hit the delete button and immediately regretted every decision she'd made in the last few weeks.

~

Daisy couldn't believe what she had just done. It was awful. Terrible. Juvenile, even. And yet she felt slightly relieved. Barring his assistant calling him near the deadline, there was a good chance that this whole deal was dead.

As the doctors walked into the room with Tristan to examine Elliana, Daisy smiled. She didn't want him to know she had anything to do with it. But she was still holding his phone behind her back, and she hoped that he didn't notice it was missing. She quickly pushed the button on the side to turn it completely off, lessening the chance that his assistant would be able to get in touch with him before midnight.

When did she become such a super spy?

She was a horrible, horrible person. This was definitely going on her permanent record. God was going to have some serious questions about this whole thing.

But the mall would not be built in her town. The land would be saved. Woodland creatures would keep their homes. And while she felt relief, she also felt sad. Why didn't it feel so good to think she would go back there and live out her life without the mall? She didn't feel nearly as happy about that as she thought she would.

"Daisy? Are you okay?"

"Oh. Yes. Sorry. I dozed off for a minute, and then my friend called me which woke me up and startled me a bit."

Now, she was just rambling. He was going to find her out if she didn't calm herself down.

"This is Dr. Morales. He's the one who just came in from Savannah."

"Nice to meet you," Daisy said, shaking the young doctor's hand.

"He's going to do a quick examination of Elliana. Do you want to walk and grab a cup of coffee with me?"

"Sure. Let me just get my bag from over here." As

she walked over to the sofa, she carefully slipped his phone back where it was and picked up her purse, for no particular reason. She really didn't need it, but she needed a ploy to walk to the sofa.

They left the room while the doctors did their work. At the end of a long hallway was a small coffee station. It wasn't the best, but it was all they had right now.

"So, what did the doctors have to say in your meeting?"

"Well, they are very optimistic that her body is responding to the antibiotics. The latest bloodwork gives them less worry about sepsis, which is good. They just have to get her through this pneumonia so we can take her back to the beach house. Hopefully that will be in the next day or so. But I want Dr. Morales to do a full examination, just to be sure he concurs."

"That's good news. I know she's going to be fine. She's a spunky, strong little girl."

They stopped at the coffee station. He poured a cup of black coffee, as expected, and she did what she always did around coffee. She loaded it with cream and sugar until it was more white than dark brown. Her grandfather used to say that her coffee could stand up in the corner by itself because it was so full of sugar.

"I want to say thanks for staying here and supporting us. I know it would've been a lot easier for you to go back to the beach house, but I really appreciate the company."

Now she really felt bad. This man trusted her, and she just let him down. But there was no going back now. Nothing she could say would make it right. She would just have to deal with the guilt and hope that everything worked out okay.

"I've enjoyed being here. I mean, I'm not enjoying Elliana being in the hospital, don't get me wrong. But it's been nice to get to know you better."

"I think I might have misjudged you at the beginning. I'm just so protective of my daughter, and that makes me a little prickly at times. I'm sorry about that. I hope we can be friends."

Friends. Why did that word hit her in a negative way? She suddenly felt like a girl in high school who had been jilted by the boy she had a crush on. Dear Lord, did she have a crush on this guy?

"There's nothing to forgive. If I had a little girl as sweet as Elliana, I would do everything to protect her, too."

"So do you think you'll ever have kids?"

That was an unexpected question. "I don't know. Maybe if I find the right person, but so far that hasn't happened."

Tristan smiled. "I find that very hard to believe."

"Why is that?"

"Well, pardon me for saying so, but you're a very

attractive woman. You're smart, very funny, quite the Monopoly player..."

"And Scrabble. Don't forget Scrabble."

"Right. You're quite the Scrabble player. I guess I would've thought guys had been flocking all around you back home. By the way, where do you come from?"

"Excuse me, Mr. Spencer? We've finished our examination and I wanted to go over some of the details. Would you mind joining us over here?"

"To be continued," he said with a wink. Wow, how could a wink make her stomach fill up with butterflies so quickly?

Daisy hurriedly walked back to the room and sat down to catch her breath. What was she supposed to say when he asked her where she was from? This was a question that she needed to come up with an answer to, and quick. It was the second time he'd asked, and the third time was evidently right around the corner.

CHAPTER 10

*D*aisy was surprised at how long it took
Tristan to get back to the room. She
worried that maybe they had some bad news about
Elliana's treatment plan or diagnosis. She tried to
find something on TV to watch that would distract
her from the little girl in the bed next to her and the
horrible thing she had done by deleting Tristan's
text message, but nothing was up to the task of that
kind of distraction.

Finally, he came through the door holding a
huge stuffed bunny rabbit and a small plastic bag.

Daisy laughed. "Wow. I guess when they say go
big or go home, you go big!"

"I can't spare anything when it comes to my little
girl. Plus, I got great news from the doctors. They
think that Elliana is already turning a corner, so I
want to make sure she has something to make her

smile as soon as she wakes up in the morning. The nurse gave her a little something to help her sleep tonight because she had been kind of restless earlier."

Daisy thought for a moment. When had she been restless? From what she had heard, Elliana was snoring most of the time. For a split second, she worried that the little girl might have heard her phone conversation with Megan, but she quickly brushed that away. What would a child of that age even understand, especially if they were in bed not feeling well?

"So, what's in the bag?"

Tristan put the stuffed rabbit next to his daughter and then walked over and sat down on the sofa. "Well, I know you said that you're not really a TV person, and this room is getting kind of boring. So, I got the only game they had in the gift shop before they closed."

He handed the bag to Daisy and she pulled out a small box. It was filled with cards, each one asking a personal question. Oh great. Just what she needed. A night filled with him grilling her about her life before she arrived in January Cove.

"Looks fun," she said, trying her best to sound like she was looking forward to her upcoming inter-rogation.

"Great. I also did something I probably wasn't supposed to do."

"What was that?"

"I ordered a pizza. I told the delivery guy to sneak up the back elevator. I offered him a pretty big tip to get it in here without us getting caught."

Daisy smiled. She liked this different part of his personality. He was starting to loosen up and trust her more.

"Well I hope you got pepperoni."

He nodded. "I just took a wild guess, but it sounds like I guessed correctly."

"You seem like you're in much better spirits tonight."

"I am. The doctors made me really feel like we would see some good progress tomorrow, especially after she gets a full night of sleep."

"I know she's going to bounce back tomorrow and be her normal, happy little self. She'll probably want us to take her to the beach or something."

"You're likely right. So, while we wait for the pizza, what do you say we start asking each other some questions?"

"Okay, I guess I'm up for that." She was totally *not* up for that. She was actually quite terrified.

They sat across from each other on separate ends of the sofa, each with their legs crossed like two little kids about to play Go Fish.

Daisy found it interesting that he was becoming so much easier to spend time with. It was like they were old friends, or maybe more, but she was trying not to think about that.

Every time she looked at him, she had to admit that her heart skipped a beat. He was a handsome guy, and it had nothing to do with the amount of money he had in his bank account. She liked him, which was surprising because she definitely had not liked him at first.

And the very fact that she liked him made her feel even more guilty about what she'd done. She'd made a huge mess of this whole situation, but she didn't have a clue how to get out of it.

"Okay, I get the first question. And it's not on one of these cards. I want to know where you're from."

She knew this was coming, and thankfully she had had time to prepare an answer. "Well, I come from a small little town in South Carolina called Cartersville. Not much there, but I love it. We have an old home place there that my grandparents built, so I like spending time on my land."

She wasn't totally lying. She didn't tell him she lived in Thornhill, the very place that he was trying to build the mall project. But the rest of her description was pretty accurate. Maybe God wouldn't strike her down with a bolt of lightning.

"Interesting. I guess I never pegged you for a small-town girl. I mean, I didn't think you were from the big city either. I think I figured a suburb?"

"A suburb, huh? I guess you could call

Cartersville a suburb. Maybe. I mean there's only about seven hundred and fifty people there, and they've all known me since birth."

Tristan laughed. "Okay, your turn. Pick a card, any card." Daisy took one from the stack.

"Here's my question for you. If you could change your profession and be anything else, what would you be?"

He thought for a moment, rubbing his chin. "I have always thought about being a veterinarian. I love dogs, especially, and I even took horse riding as a kid. But I was chubby, and I kept sliding off the horse."

Daisy laughed loudly and then covered her mouth so as not to wake every patient on the hallway. "You were chubby? I can't imagine that at all."

"Really? Because I'm so sexy now?" He pretended to flex his muscles. Dang, he really did have some nice muscles. "I think maybe I'd be a large animal vet."

Daisy smiled. "That is a shocking answer. I don't think I pegged you as an animal lover."

"You know, it really makes me sad that you have thought so little of me, apparently. Who doesn't love animals?"

"A lot of people don't love animals! People are scared of dogs, horses, even cats. You just seem a little more... put together. I can't imagine you cleaning up puppy poop or taking a horse's temperature."

Tristan chuckled. "Well, I probably would hire someone to clean the puppy poop, as you call it. I've actually always wanted to have some kind of animal sanctuary, you know, where I could save animals that are injured or nobody wants."

"That's amazing. You have the means to do it, so why haven't you?"

He thought for a moment. "You know, I'm not sure why. I guess I've just been so hyper focused on my business that it didn't seem like a priority. But I think maybe it's something I'll look into."

"Then this game has been worth it."

He smiled. There was a moment between them, a flash of something that Daisy couldn't put her finger on immediately. But then they were interrupted by a nurse bringing a very concerned looking young pizza delivery man into the room.

"Mr. Spencer, did you really bribe this young boy to bring you pizza?" she said, her Southern drawl apparent.

Tristan stood and shrugged his shoulders. "We were hungry."

The nurse laughed. "Well, I work until six AM, so I'll tell you what. I won't say anything as long as you give me a slice of that pizza."

They all laughed, except for the pizza delivery

guy who still looked like he was afraid he was going to jail.

Tristan quickly paid the guy and slipped him a tip. The young man looked down, grinned from ear to ear and darted out of the door like someone was going to catch him in a butterfly net.

Tristan opened the box and allowed the nurse to take a piece of the pizza before closing the door behind her.

He turned to Daisy and held out the box. "Boy, she drives a hard bargain."

Daisy took one of the napkins and a large piece of pizza. She was starving. Her eating had been very erratic in the last couple of days given that the hospital cafeteria's food was less than edible.

"Alright, back to our game. So I guess it's my turn again."

He held the pizza in one hand and slid a card out of the stack with the other.

"I'm scared, but go ahead."

"My question for you is what is the scariest moment you've ever had?"

She wanted to say this one. Or the time that she pretended to be a nanny and showed up at a billionaire's door. But those were not exactly things she could share with him, so she wracked her brain for something else.

"When I was a kid, we used to have this area near our house where wildflowers grew during the spring. One day, I was out there picking wildflowers with my friend who was a couple of years younger than me. I was only about nine years old. This man pulled up in a dark vehicle and got out. He was carrying this black leather bag. I was kind of a scared kid anyway, and I was convinced he was coming to kidnap us so I grabbed my friend's arm and we took off running as fast as we could."

"Oh my gosh! What happened?"

"Well, the guy chased us. He was running really fast, and we were small so we had a hard time getting away. We headed straight into my house without saying a word to my grandmother, and went into my bedroom and locked the door."

"Did they catch the guy?" Tristan was leaning forward, totally mesmerized by her story.

"Well, that's where the story gets kind of funny. The guy came to our front door and talked to my grandmother. Turns out, he worked for the local newspaper and had just moved to town so I didn't recognize him. He was just trying to get our picture picking the spring flowers."

Tristan started laughing. "You should be a writer. You really had me on the edge of my seat for that story."

"Kind of an anti-climactic ending, but it was definitely scary for us."

"Okay, your turn again."

She finished her slice of pizza, wiped her hands

on the napkin and reached for another card. This game wasn't as scary as she had worried it might be.

"You're question is what do you see yourself doing five years from now?"

Tristan's face almost had a sadness on it. She couldn't peg exactly what he was thinking.

"My daughter will be thirteen years old. A teenager. That's incredibly hard to imagine. I feel like I'll probably be beating boys off with a stick by then. But, as for me, I don't know. Working, I guess?"

"You seem a little sad about that."

"I don't know, I guess I don't wanna spend my entire life working or what was it all for? But I have a really hard time taking time out to just enjoy life."

"Isn't that what you're doing right now?"

He sat there quietly for a moment. "It is. I sort of got forced into it by the situation with my daughter, and I don't want her to be sick like this ever again. But yes, I guess it's nice to take a little time out and not focus on my business."

"So... five years from now?"

"I don't know. I guess I hope to find someone I can share my life with who loves my daughter and who will call me on my crap so I don't waste my life away working."

Daisy's heart started to pound. There was something going on between them. He stared at her for quite some time before they were interrupted by the nurse coming in to check Elliana's vitals.

Maybe this game was more dangerous than she thought.

~

They sat there for well over an hour, asking each other questions, laughing and re-counting old memories. To Tristan, it felt a lot like a great date with a high school girlfriend or something. Not at all like the dates he went on in recent years, mostly with women who were only interested in him because of how many zeros were in his bank account.

At the same time, he was still struggling with the fact that he was growing more and more attached and interested in a woman who was only going to be there temporarily. He couldn't risk getting his daughter's feelings hurt by losing another person in her life.

And he didn't think his heart could take it either.

But still, she seemed to have everything he wanted. She was down to earth, beautiful but in an understated way, funny, smart, even a little bit sarcastic. There was nothing about her that was false or putting up a front. She was just so authentic.

He felt like the more he talked to her, the more the layers of himself were stripping away. He was no longer just "the billionaire" or the guy who had made the front page of Forbes magazine several months ago. Did she even know that? Would she even care?

Everything they talked about revolved around real life and real feelings. She never asked much about his business, apart from that mall project he had mentioned to her briefly.

And when the clock passed midnight, it was only then that he realized that his phone had apparently died at some point during the day. Never once had he thought about checking his email or his texts. Not only was his little girl laying in a hospital bed, which made business completely outside of his comprehension for a while, but he was so mesmerized with the woman in front of him that he didn't really care what was going on in his business right now.

And that made him feel incredibly uncomfortable and scared. If he was honest with himself, he wanted to make a move. Maybe put his arm around her or kiss her on the cheek or even just touch her hand again. But he had no idea if she was even interested. Maybe he was concocting all of this in his head. But a part of him thought she might be interested too as they had shared a few electric moments.

Now it was time to go to bed so that both of them would be refreshed in the morning when Elliana hopefully woke up feeling better. But there was one problem - all they had was this very hard, fairly small built-in sofa. Maybe he should offer to take her back to the house for the night or see if they could bring in some extra chairs that he could make into some kind of bed for himself.

"I'm getting pretty tired. I'm sure you are too."

"Yeah, I think we both need some quality rest for tomorrow. Hopefully we will wake up to her bright, smiling face," she said. Just hearing her talk about his daughter in that way made him well up inside.

"So, how do you want to do this? I really don't mind if you want to go back to the beach house or something."

Daisy yawned. "I think I'd be uncomfortable there by myself, honestly."

Tristan smiled. "It's a gated community, Daisy."

"And there are sharks in the ocean right behind the house, *Tristan*." The emphasis she put on his name made him chuckle.

"I don't think they've quite mastered walking on land yet."

She opened a cabinet in the corner of the room and pulled out a pillow and blanket. "You never know." She handed the blanket and pillow to Tristan.

"Why are you giving me this?"

"I'm going to go ask the nurse for a chair. I'm small. I can prop my feet on the foot of the bed and sleep like that."

He rolled his eyes. "What kind of a guy do you think I am that I'd let a woman sleep in a chair while I slept on this glorious sofa?"

"Well, you certainly can't sleep in the chair. You're way too tall."

The nurse came in to check Elliana's IV, so Tristan took the chance to ask her about sleeping arrangements.

"Sorry, Mr. Spencer, but the hospital is at capacity with this flu. But, that sofa does make out into a small bed. Just pull on these straps here..." She pulled it out, revealing the extra space. It was still small, but better than just a sofa. "Should be plenty for you and your wife."

Tristan coughed. "Oh, we're not married."

"Sorry. You and your fiancee."

He shook his head.

"Girlfriend? Look, I don't judge how people choose to live their lives..."

Daisy giggled. "I'm his nanny. Well, not *his* nanny. I'm Elliana's nanny."

The nurse, an older African American woman with quite a personality, looked between the two of them and smiled. "Whatever you say. Goodnight, folks." She closed the door, leaving them alone again.

"Well, I guess there's enough space for both of us now," Daisy finally said. "You like left or right?"

"Left."

"Oh."

"You like left too?"

"It's fine..."

Tristan put his hands on her shoulders and looked down into her eyes. "You take the left."

She stared up at him, her eyes wide. Did she feel that too? Did she know there was something between them that was more than employer and employee? All he knew was that he didn't want to remove his hands from her shoulders, but he did.

The touch of his hands on her shoulders had sent shivers up and down her body. How in the world was she supposed to lay in a bed next to him? Had he noticed the goosebumps that trailed up and down her body every time he got too close?

The nurse brought them an extra pillow and blanket, thankfully. The last thing she needed was to be sharing a pillow and snuggling under one small hospital blanket.

They each laid down, both staring at the ceiling. The only light in the room was a small emergency light near the door, the blinking light on Elliana's IV machine and the moonlight streaming in from the window behind their heads.

"Why can't I sleep if I'm so tired?" Tristan said after a few minutes.

"Adrenaline. You've been scared since yesterday, so you probably needed to take a good brisk walk before bed to get it out of your system."

"Do you think I'd get in trouble if I sprinted down the hall then?"

Daisy laughed. "I wouldn't chance it."

"What if we ask more questions to each other?"

Oh no. She'd gotten out of that unscathed before, but could she go for a second round?

"Fine. Just for a few minutes, and then you really need to get some sleep."

"Yes, Mom," he said. Without thinking, she used her shoulder to bump into his. It was hard to remember that he was still her boss, no matter how chummy they were in the present moment.

"All right, my question for you is this - what kind of man are you looking for?"

Daisy got very still. Why was he asking her a question like that? Was he having the same feelings about her as she was having about him? Thank God he couldn't see the redness that was moving across her face.

"Well, I've never really thought a lot about it, but I guess I'm looking for someone who is kind, honest, loyal..."

"Forgive me for saying so, but you sound like you're talking about what kind of rescue dog you want."

She turned up on her side, barely able to make out the stubble along his jaw line that she liked to look at so much. "I guess there's something to be said for the loyalty of a rescue dog. Why is that a bad thing to look for in a man?"

Tristan turned to face her, and he was dangerously close. There were only a few inches separating their faces, and with darkness and closeness, that wasn't a good combination.

"You can find a friend who is loyal and honest and kind. What kind of a *man* do you want?" he repeated.

"Good looking. Stable. Comforting. A good provider. Is that better?"

"Yes, that's a lot better," he whispered, his voice low.

"What about you?"

"Well, I'm not actually looking for a man."

Daisy laughed. "You know what I mean."

"Well, obviously, she has to be beautiful because if I'm going to spend my life with her, I need someone nice to look at."

"Typical guy."

"Well you wouldn't want to look at a troll for the rest of your life, would you?" he said, trying to be funny.

"We can't all be beautiful, but please continue."

"I guess I'm looking for someone who will inspire me, encourage me and be my biggest cheerleader and confidante. I want someone who isn't just interested in my bank account, but cares about me as a person. I want someone who will love my daughter the way I do, and who will protect her when I'm not around. I want someone who will be my best friend."

She was realizing more and more how deep he really was. What must it be like to not know who you can trust just because of how much money you have, she wondered. And here he was trusting her, and she'd done nothing but lie since the day they met. He didn't really know her at all, and that made her feel awful. She was just going to be another woman who betrayed his trust. The thought made her feel sick.

"You okay? Was my answer too silly?" he asked.

"No, it wasn't silly at all. I was just thinking about how it must be hard for you to know who to trust, with all of your money, I mean."

"Yeah, it's very hard. Having money is great, but having someone you can trust to share it with would be a true gift."

She felt a stray tear fall from her eye and was thankful for the darkness. More than anything, she wished she could take it all back. Of course, that would've meant never meeting Tristan Spencer, but to save him the heartache of ever meeting her would've been worth it. She didn't deserve a guy like him giving her a second look. When had she become such a liar?

"I'm feeling pretty tired. I think I'm going to turn in now," she said, trying desperately not to break into sobs.

"Okay. Me too," he said, falling back onto his back. Daisy turned to face the other direction.

"Goodnight."

"Goodnight," he said. "Oh, and Daisy? I think you're one beautiful woman."

Ugh. Life wasn't fair.

CHAPTER 11

*D*aisy awoke with a start, her body feeling immobile. She'd had incidences of sleep paralysis as a kid, but none since being an adult. Was that what was happening? She couldn't move her legs at all, and her body felt warm. Her eyes would barely open because she was so tired.

As she started to come to her senses, she realized where she was. The hospital room. The incredibly hard and uncomfortable "bed". It was still pitch black dark, with only a sliver of moonlight that allowed her to see. She tried to move, but felt like a lead weight was on her body.

And then she remembered that Tristan was lying next to her. No, he was partially lying *on* her. She was facing away from him and he was holding her like a large stuffed animal with one arm draped over her upper half and his leg draped over hers.

She was trapped, and it felt wonderful. Of

course, he was sound asleep, lightly snoring in her ear, his warm breath cascading down her neck. He had no idea, of course, what he was doing. Should she wake him up? Disrupt his sleep? Possibly embarrass him and make things awkward for a few weeks?

Daisy thought better of it and laid there, enjoying the closeness of a man she was finding herself more and more attracted to each day. But she couldn't pursue it. She'd lied to him, and no relationship could be built on lies.

Still, she couldn't feel her legs and her arm was falling asleep. She had to move. She didn't want to wake him, so she wiggled until she was able to turn onto her back. Feeling the blood finally running back into her legs and arm, she relaxed. Tristan never moved. She thought about how tired he must be, both physically and emotionally from worrying about his daughter.

She still wasn't quite comfortable, so against her better judgment, she turned toward him. He started to rouse, a moan escaping his lips. In the moonlight, she could see his eyes flutter open and then close. Thinking she'd managed to get comfortable without waking him up, she closed her eyes in an attempt to drift back off to sleep.

And then it happened. She felt his lips softly press against hers, and her eyes popped open. He then let out a sigh and fell onto his back, his arm and leg pulling away from her.

He'd kissed her in his sleep.

What did that mean? And how would she ever kiss another man after that one? If that was how he kissed when he was asleep, what would an awake kiss feel like?

Daisy got little sleep for the rest of the night. Instead, she listened to Tristan lightly snore, relived the sleepy kiss he'd given her and wondered what to do next.

Morning came awfully early, Tristan thought. It didn't feel like he'd slept a wink before the rising sun infiltrated the room. Of course, the constant comings and goings of the nurse throughout the night hadn't helped him sleep soundly.

Elliana seemed to still be sleeping, and Daisy looked so peaceful next to him. She was facing him, her hands under her cheek. How was it that she still looked so beautiful after the couple of days they'd been through?

Beautiful. Oh my gosh. Had he actually told her she was beautiful? What kind of a boss did that?

Still, he had to admit he'd had pleasant dreams about her last night, the best one ending in an unforgettable kiss.

He had to stop this. It was never going to happen.

She was working for him, and maybe he was making her uncomfortable telling her things about being beautiful.

"Good morning," she said, her voice raspy and a little sexy.

"Good morning. Sleep well?"

"As well as one can on a stack of two by fours," she said, pushing up onto her elbows. "Honestly, where did they get this cushion? It feels like it's full of concrete."

Tristan laughed. "Yeah, not exactly a five star hotel. But thanks for staying with me."

They both sat up and stretched. "Wonder when the doctor's coming by?"

"I'm not sure. I think I'll go check if you don't mind staying here?"

"Not as long as you grab some coffee?"

He smiled. "We're getting into a routine. I kind of like it."

She returned his smile. "So do I."

As he walked out of the room, he had renewed hope that maybe she was feeling something too.

Daisy dug through her small backpack looking for makeup and deodorant. Being at the hospital in the same clothes for a couple of days was starting to make her feel gross. Maybe she'd offer to go back to the house and get some necessities for them if Elliana was going to need to stay another night.

"Daisy?"

She turned to see Elliana sitting up in her bed, rubbing her eyes.

"Elliana! I'm so happy to see you awake!" Daisy ran over and sat on the edge of the bed. "How are you feeling?"

"I can breathe better. Where's my Daddy?"

"He went to find the doctor and get us some coffee, but he'll be right back."

Elliana turned and saw the stuffed bunny in her bed. "Where did this come from?"

"Your Daddy bought it for you last night. He's been so worried. I know he's going to be so excited to see you sitting up!"

"I'm ready to get out of here. Can we go soon?"

"The doctor is going to come and check you over real good. Then we'll know more."

"Okay, but I'm starving too."

"I know you must be, sweetie. As soon as the doctor checks you, we'll get you something yummy to eat, okay?"

Before Elliana could respond, Tristan came back into the room. When he saw his daughter sitting up, a big smile spread across his face. He put the cups of coffee down on the rolling table next to her bed.

"Elliana! Oh my gosh, honey, it's so good to see

you sitting up!" he said as he ran over to the bed and pulled her into a hug.

"Ouch!" she said, pointing to her little arm that still held the IV that seemed way too large for her veins.

"Sorry, sweetie. I was just so excited to see you."

"When can we get out of here? I really wanted to pick up more seashells." Her voice was still weak, and she was a little groggy, but Daisy felt such relief.

Tristan looked at Daisy and they both laughed. The little girl was oblivious to how dangerous her situation had been. Just like a child, she really only wanted to get back to her regular life of picking up seashells and playing at the waters' edge.

"Well, I just talked to the doctor and he's very happy about your progress. But, he wants you to stay one more night just to be on the safe side."

Elliana groaned and laid back against her pillow, her bottom lip jutting out.

Daisy was a little disappointed to hear that also. She wanted Elliana to be healthy when she left the hospital, but she also longed for a nice hot shower and a comfortable bed. It was amazing how just a couple of days of discomfort could get to a person.

"I'm really hungry."

"Well, the doctor did say that we could get you a good lunch outside of the hospital, so why don't I run out and get you something?"

"No, don't do that. You stay here with her and I'll

go get us some food. But if you don't mind, I'd love to run by the house first and get a quick shower, freshen up..."

Tristan smiled. "Of course. Maybe I could convince you to pick up a few things for me?"

"Sure. No problem."

A few minutes later, Daisy left the hospital and made her way back to the beach house. She wanted to hurry because she knew Elliana was starving. They had decided to pick up sandwiches from the shop they'd heard good things about on the main street. Daisy also wanted to go by Jolt, the popular local coffee shop, and get some decent coffee for her and Tristan.

She went into the beach house, packed up the things she needed and went into Tristan's room. Everything was so organized, unlike herself. She had things strewn all over her room like a crazed teenager. And he had all of his things nicely hung in the closet and folded in the drawers like he'd moved into the place permanently.

She looked at the list he had given her and quickly packed his things into the same bag with hers.

She took off her clothes, jumped into the shower and took the quickest shower she'd ever taken in her life. Before departing, she thought it would be a good time to call Megan and catch her up on everything that had happened.

"So you ended up deleting the text after all?" Megan said, disappointment in her voice.

"Look, it's over and done with. I feel horrible. I can't tell you how immediately regretful I was."

"Then why didn't you just 'fess up? Why didn't you just tell him what you'd done?"

"Because if I do that, my entire cover is blown. I don't want to hurt that little girl or him. It's better if they just never know what happened. I mean, I'm sure he's got tons of deals, so he'll just move on to something else."

"You better hope so. I think you could get into some real trouble for this, Daisy. It's gone way too far."

"I know, I know."

"Do you? Because I've been trying to talk you out of this the entire time. Honestly, I thought you would chicken out before you even got to the front door. I never thought you would let it go this far."

"I think I just let it get the best of me. Plus, this guy is so nice and good looking. It's hard to wanna leave. So I'm just going to finish doing my job and try to get out of here without him finding out what a horrific person I am."

"So you slept in the same bed last night?"

"I don't think I would exactly call it a bed. It's the hardest built-in sofa you've ever seen that pulls out slightly to allow two people to lay down."

"And how did that go?"

"Well..."

"Wait. Did something happen?"

"Kind of. I woke up in the middle of the night with his leg and arm wrapped around me. He was totally asleep. I tried to readjust because I lost feeling in my limbs and when I turned on my side, he kissed me in his sleep."

"Are you sure he was asleep?"

"Yes. Totally asleep. Has no recollection from what I can tell. But I have to say, I've been kissed by a few guys before, and this guy kisses better in his sleep than any guy I've ever kissed awake."

Megan laughed. "You sure have gotten yourself into a pickle, haven't you?"

"That's an understatement."

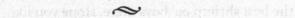

When Daisy arrived back at the hospital, she walked into the room to see Tristan sitting in the bed with Elliana, reading her a book. She looked alert and almost back to herself, which was a huge relief.

"Oh, hey," Tristan said when he saw her. There was a familiarity in his tone, and her mind immediately flashed back to the kiss he didn't know they had. Suddenly, she found herself daydreaming about coming home from work in the evenings, the both of them enjoying a glass of wine while sitting on the terrace of his penthouse. Of course, she didn't know if he even had a penthouse, but where else did billionaires live?

"Hey," she said. "And look at you, Elliana! Your cheeks are rosy again."

"What does rosy mean?"

Tristan chuckled. "It means you're looking more like yourself, and we are both so happy about that."

Daisy walked to the sofa and put down the bags. "Okay, so I got us both some clothes. I also went by the bookstore, and I got Elliana a couple of coloring books and some coloring supplies. The front desk said we can rent her some movies on the TV here, so here's the flyer showing what they have. Lots of Disney stuff, of course. I picked up sandwiches from Skeeter's down by the ferry station. I heard they have the best shrimp po' boys there. Hope you like shrimp... I got Elliana a grilled cheese from their children's menu..." she continued rattling off the snacks she'd brought as she dug through her backpack and the reusable shopping bags she'd loaded full at the grocery store too.

When she stopped talking and took a deep breath, she looked over at Tristan. He had a bemused look on his face.

"What?"

"I'm just a little amazed, I guess. How did you manage to throw all of that together in the short time you were gone?"

Daisy shrugged her shoulders. "I don't know. I guess I can be a bit energetic when I need to be. Anyway, here you go, sweetie. Color to your heart's content." She handed the supplies and sandwich to Elliana, who immediately dug into the bag. Tristan joined Daisy by the window.

"Seriously, thank you. I know she's bored, so having that stuff will keep her occupied for awhile." He took a sandwich from the brown paper bag and sat down. Daisy joined him. "You'll make a great mother one day, Daisy."

Her heart fluttered. It did that a lot around him. "Another night, huh?" she said.

"Hopefully just the one."

"I guess we'll make the best of it. Sure you don't want me to stay here so you can get a good night's sleep at the beach house?" she offered.

Tristan smiled, a chunk of his sandwich poking out one cheek. "I'm sure. Last night was... nice. You didn't think so?"

Her stomach felt like it was falling down a flight of stairs. "I... um... yes. I enjoyed it. I mean, this sofa stinks as far as comfort goes..."

"I wasn't actually referring to the sofa," he said, studying her face in a way that made her shift uncomfortably in her seat.

"Oh."

"Can I tell you a little secret?" he whispered, making sure Elliana couldn't hear them.

"Of course."

"This is kind of embarrassing... I had a dream about you last night."

"Oh really?" Her heart rate started to speed up. "What was it about?"

"Well, I don't really remember, actually. I think we were on the pier. We were taking a walk at sunset. And..."

"And?"

He was struggling not to smile, his cheeks turning a bit crimson in the process. "I think we kissed."

Daisy bit her lip. "Really? Interesting. And how did that go?"

Tristan smiled. "Very, very well."

"I'm thirsty," Elliana called from her bed. Tristan chuckled, rolled his eyes and sighed before getting up to give her a juice box.

"Good afternoon, folks," Dr. Morales said as he entered the room.

"Oh, hey, doc," Tristan replied as he held the juice box up to Elliana's mouth while she colored with one hand and held her sandwich in the other.

"Well, look at you, little lady! You're looking much better today. I do believe we'll get you home tomorrow."

"What a relief," Daisy said. She was surprised at how much she'd grown to love Elliana already. She hadn't expected that.

Tristan smiled at her and then turned back to the doctor.

"I just want to do a follow up x-ray to make sure that the pneumonia is responding like we think it is. Care to take a little walk with my nurse, Elliana?"

"Okay..." she said, reluctantly putting down her sandwich and crayons. The nurse helped her climb out of bed.

"We just want to make sure she can get around okay and breathe well before we send her home. Nurse Sheila here is going to take you on a little walk and then to get an x-ray. I'll touch base with you folks later this afternoon, okay?"

Tristan nodded as the doctor, the nurse and Elliana all left the room. Now they were alone. Daisy's pulse quickened again. Maybe she needed to get herself checked by a doctor too.

He walked over to the sofa and sat down, a slight smile on his face as he looked at Daisy. She looked down, like some kind of shy middle school girl, and then joined him on the sofa.

"So, it was a good dream, huh?" she finally said.

"Very, very good, actually."

They sat in silence for a few moments. "I have no idea what to say."

Tristan chuckled. "Neither do I. This isn't something I'm exactly used to."

She looked at him. "What do you mean?"

"Feelings like this."

"Surely, you've had girlfriends?"

He smiled, that darned dimple capturing her attention yet again. "Many."

"Of course."

"But the last woman I had actual feelings for, besides Elliana's mother, was my short-term high school girlfriend, Sadie."

"What happened to her?"

"We broke up when she fell for the school's quarterback. They got married and have six kids, last I heard."

"Wow."

"Yeah."

"So, what about all of the other girlfriends?"

"I tend to attract fake women who are more interested in the size of my wallet."

"And this?" she asked, pointing between the two of them.

He looked at her, his gaze impossible to break away from. "I don't know what to do with *this*. It's a foreign feeling to me. I'm always focused on work, and this feels like a subject I never studied in college and now I'm supposed to take the final exam, but I don't know any of the answers."

"Tristan, are you saying you're interested in... dating me?" She was terrified asking the question. What if she was totally mis-reading the situation?

"Maybe. I don't know. I mean, it's kind of a weird situation..."

"Right. I totally understand. And you're right..."

He reached over and squeezed her hand for a moment before letting go. "I didn't say no, Daisy." She smiled, longing for him to lean over and kiss her, like in one of those chick flicks Megan had forced her to watch a million times. "I will say that you make me forget to work, and that's never happened before."

"I'm not sure if that's a good thing or a bad thing?" Daisy said laughing.

"Oh, no... I totally forgot to check in with my assistant last night." Tristan leaned over and picked up his phone from the table. "I charged it all night but it's not coming on... wait, how did I manage to turn it off? No wonder he didn't call me..."

Daisy's heart sped up again, but this time for fear of getting caught in her web of lies.

"I need to make a call. Do you mind?"

"Of course not."

Tristan stood and crossed the room. "Curt? Hey. What? No... Elliana was sick. We've been in the hospital... Yeah, she's getting better... Wait. What? The mall project? No, I never got a text..." He pulled the phone from his ear and looked through his text messages. "Deadline? We missed it? But... You're kidding me! Are you freaking kidding me? Oh man..."

The irritation and aggravation in his voice made Daisy feel so bad. What kind of person was she? And now he had feelings... and she had feelings... and feelings were dangerous, especially when they were built on lies.

He ended the call and stared off into the distance. "I can't believe it."

"What's wrong?"

"That mall project... There was a deadline last night that I didn't know about... my phone somehow got turned off, so I didn't get the text... The deal's dead. Someone else got it and turned it into conservation land."

Daisy stood, running her hands down her thighs to keep him from seeing her hands shake. "Jeez, I'm sorry, Tristan. That stinks."

"Yeah. I need a little time alone, if you don't mind. I think I'll take a walk, blow off some steam. Can you wait here for Elliana?"

"Sure."

He left the room without looking back. Did he suspect her? Daisy sank down onto the sofa and fell forward, her head in her hands. She'd made a real mess of this, that much was sure.

CHAPTER 12

Tristan walked back-and-forth on the sidewalk outside of the hospital. He just didn't understand how this could've possibly happened. The deal was a sure thing, and now it was gone.

It wasn't like he needed the money or anything. But he hated to lose. Especially when it was a deal he had been working on for months.

This had to have something to do with the environmental group, he thought. Somebody must've had the inside track. This didn't happen by accident. The question was, how much effort did he want to put into figuring it out?

Truthfully, he felt a little bit of relief. The deal was going to be very time-consuming and require a lot of travel for the next couple of years. After what happened with his daughter, did he really want to invest that kind of time?

If nothing else, this whole situation had taught him to appreciate the time he had with Elliana. He definitely had not been doing that recently.

And then there was Daisy. He had strong feelings that he didn't expect. But was it because they were in such an emotional situation at the hospital? Or was it because she was the right woman for him?

He had no idea. He thought back and tried to remember how strong his feelings were before his daughter got sick. Was he imagining all of these great things about her? Or was she really the other half he'd been looking for?

He sat down on a concrete bench under a large magnolia tree. There was just something about her that made him feel happy and fulfilled. She truly did make him forget about work, and no woman on the planet had ever been able to accomplish that.

He liked to watch Daisy with his daughter. She was very motherly, although she probably didn't realize it. He could see the love in her eyes when she looked at Elliana, and that made him want to scoop her up and never let her go.

But that was the problem. She was his employee, even if only temporarily. How would they ever make something like this work?

He couldn't hire her to be the full-time nanny at home and then date her at same time. That was gross and inappropriate.

But he also couldn't ask her to uproot her life

and come live closer to him. Why was he thinking things like this anyway? They weren't even a couple!

Maybe he was thinking too far ahead. He had a tendency to do that. He always tried to figure out every possibility and eventuality, and come up with solutions before there were problems.

But right now, all he felt was this butterfly feeling in the pit of his stomach that he'd never felt before. *This must be what people talk about when they fall in love*, he thought. Suddenly, every chick flick he'd been forced to watch made sense.

Even with Elliana's mother, although he'd thought he loved her, he never felt like this. All he knew right now was that he wanted to get his daughter out of the hospital, get them all back to the beach house and try to sort out his feelings. Something told him this wasn't going to be as easy as he might hope.

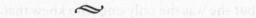

The rest of the afternoon was spent with Elliana, alternately watching silly animated movies and playing card games. The doctors were very pleased with her progress and felt like one more night at the hospital was all she would need. As long as she passed all of their tests the next day, they would be on their way back to the beach house.

Daisy was surprised at how tired a person could

get just hanging around the hospital. She did stretches, occasionally did squats to get her blood moving and took a couple of walks down the hall, mostly to ooh and ahh over the babies in the nursery.

The people that worked at the hospital were some of the nicest that she had ever met. Even being from a small town herself, she was surprised at how cordial and welcoming everyone was in January Cove. She could see herself living in a place like this, even though the ocean was right there, taunting her.

But, somehow, she wasn't nearly as scared of it as she had been when she arrived. Or maybe it was just that she wasn't as scared of life now that she knew Tristan. In a strange way, it felt like she finally had someone who truly had her back.

And then she reminded herself that she wasn't trustworthy and he really didn't know who she was anyway. This was all a charade. This was all pretend, but she was the only one who knew that.

But her feelings were not pretend, and that was causing so many conflicting emotions that she had a hard time keeping up.

She tried to think of ways that she could get out of the situation without him ever knowing what she'd done. She wondered if there was a way to still have that perfect, picket fence ending without him ever realizing she was as deceitful as she had been.

She felt horrible for not just confessing right

now. But if she did that, so many dominoes would fall and so many people would get hurt that it didn't seem worth it. Her only hope was to get out of town at the end of summer and hope that Tristan never sat down and really connected the dots.

"Are you tired?" Tristan asked Elliana as he stood over her bed, squeezing her knee.

"Yes. I'm very tired," she said, groggily, her eyes closing over and over like lead weights were weighing them down.

"Why don't you go ahead and get some sleep. We'll turn off the TV, and tomorrow morning we'll hopefully be heading back to enjoy the rest of our vacation." He pulled the cover up around her neck and kissed her forehead.

Within a few minutes, she was peacefully snoring. Tristan sat down on the sofa next to Daisy and they both sighed at the same time.

"I'm so glad this is almost over. I pray that her tests check out tomorrow so that we can get back to enjoying the summer. I certainly didn't expect this for my daughter."

"Everything is going to be fine." Daisy was saying it as much for him as for herself. It was times like these when she missed her grandparents and their calming demeanor. Of course, her grandmother would've slapped her upside the head by now for doing such a stupid thing. Her grandfather would've known how to stop the mall deal before it even started. He was smart about those things, and he was always in control. Never had she met a man who was more calm in a crisis than her beloved Papa.

"So, what should we do now? I'm not exactly ready to fall asleep. How about you?"

"Not really. What about maybe taking a walk outside? Stretch our legs a bit?" Daisy stood, hoping he'd say yes.

Tristan looked over at his daughter. "I guess that would be okay. I'll ask one of the nurses to come sit with her. Things seem to be pretty quiet out there."

Daisy smiled. "I'm pretty sure those nurses will do whatever you ask."

"One of the perks of being who I am. I'm not going to complain this time." He winked at her, and her legs started to feel like Jell-O. What was it about him that made her swoon? She had never understood what swooning was until she met Tristan.

The nurse agreed to come in and watch Elliana for a little while. They walked downstairs and out onto the sidewalk. Daisy was so happy to get some fresh air. The hospital was not exactly the most exciting place to hang out for days at a time.

"It's beautiful out here."

"It is. I love the feel of the constant ocean breeze. I've often thought about moving to the beach," Tristan said.

They walked slowly along the sidewalk, under

the massive magnolia trees that were out in front of the grounds.

"Yeah, I could kind of see myself living here."

Tristan stopped in his tracks, his mouth hanging open. "Did Daisy Davenport just say that she was thinking about living near the ocean?"

"I didn't say for sure. I'm just saying that I wouldn't rule it out."

Tristan smiled and started walking again. "That's huge progress, though. Why aren't you as afraid of it anymore?"

She took in a deep breath and blew it out slowly. "I don't know really. I guess you holding my hands on the dolphin cruise just gave me a sense of peace. I mean I'm not going scuba diving or snorkeling anytime soon, but I wouldn't rule out walking along the edge of the ocean and getting my feet wet from time to time."

He stopped again, a big grin on his face. "I'm so glad you said that. Why don't we do that right now?"

"You're not serious?"

"Why not?"

"Because it's pitch black dark and there's all kinds of weird critters on the beach at night. And... Well I can't think of another reason right now, but give me a minute..."

He took her arm and gently started pulling her toward the crosswalk. "No time like the present!"

"Tristan, I don't think this is a good idea..."

"I think it's a fantastic idea. It'll be a full circle moment. Do it for Elliana."

"Now, that isn't fair," she said, laughing as he pulled her across the street and down a small public pathway to the beach.

All she could hear was the crashing of the waves in the distance. Nothing was visible but the black night, the moonlight reflecting off the water and the white caps of the waves hitting the shore.

"And what if one of those little crabs runs across my feet?" she asked.

"Then I'll scoop you up and carry you until we reach safety," he said laughing.

She suddenly started hoping to see crabs.

"Take off your shoes," Tristan said as he kicked off his canvas boat shoes and walked toward the water. Reluctantly, Daisy kicked off her sandals and followed him. As they got closer, she stopped and stood still, staring out into what she considered the black abyss of death.

"I don't think I can do this," she said, truly scared of what might be lurking even in a few inches of water. Tristan stopped, turned around and looked at her, empathy in his eyes.

"I would never let anything bad happen to you. You know that, right?"

Suddenly, Daisy felt like she wanted to cry. Not only because she had deceived him, but because he reminded her so much of her grandfather in that moment. The same sort of peace she got from being around her Papa suddenly flowed over her yet again. Maybe her grandfather had sent this man to her.

"I believe you," she said as she tried to summon the courage to walk forward. He reached out his hand.

"I won't let go of your hand. I promise."

She nodded and took his hand, feeling the warmth of his fingers wrap around hers. Oh this was bad for so many different reasons...

They walked toward the water, and she felt the first tendrils of the warm liquid touching her toes. It felt unexpectedly peaceful. No one was around, not even one person. All she could see in the distance was the occasional light on in a house behind her or an illuminated boat off in the distance. It felt like they were the only two people on earth.

Tristan went further into the water as she stayed closer to safety, but she was doing it. She was really walking in the ocean. And he was really holding her hand. Right now, she was more scared of him letting go than she was anything that might be in the water.

"I'm so proud of you," he said. She could actually hear the pride in his voice.

"I am pretty proud of myself, to be honest. I can't believe I'm doing this."

They walked along quietly for a while. After all, they couldn't go very far. Tristan occasionally looked back to make sure he could still see the hospital just so they didn't get too far away from Elliana.

"We can go back whenever you're ready," Daisy said.

"I don't think she's going to wake up until morning. And I'm not quite ready to go back yet. I need to blow off a little steam."

"Oh yeah? And how are you going to do that?"

"Do you mind if I let go of your hand for just a minute?"

"Sure. I'm just going to take a seat over here on the sand and watch the show." She didn't know what he was going to do, but she certainly wasn't getting involved. Just walking on a dark beach was plenty scary enough for her. She didn't need to blow off any steam.

Without warning, he suddenly dropped his phone and keys next to her, peeled off his shirt and ran out into the water.

"Tristan! You're going to get eaten by a shark! Or one of those little crabs is going to bite me! Get back over here!"

She could hear him laughing in the distance. All she could see was the moonlight reflecting off of his head as he dove underwater and came back up. He looked like some kind of Greek god coming out of the water, the streams of white light showcasing every muscle in his chest and arms.

"Do you want to join me?" he called to her.

"I'm going to have to give you a big, fat no on that one!" she yelled back, laughing.

For a few moments, he dove in and out of the water like some kind of psychotic dolphin. When he finally rode the last wave back into shore, he flopped down beside her on his back, breathing hard.

"You're crazy," she said, slapping him on the arm. "And now what are you going to do for clothes?"

"Well, you see, that's the beauty of the beach. By the time we get back to the hospital, these shorts will be all dried out."

"I suppose you're right. We have a little bit of a walk ahead of us."

"I'm still out of breath. I obviously need to do more cardio when I get back home."

"Are you looking forward to going home?"

"I don't know. I like it here. I wasn't expecting that. I go on a lot of trips, and normally I'm just ready to get back to work when I get home. But this time, I don't know, something's different."

"Oh yeah? What do you think that is?"

He sat up, his forearms resting on his knees. "I think the difference is you."

"I don't live in January Cove."

"I'm not sure January Cove is the reason why I don't want to leave this place. Look, I don't understand these feelings I've been having. At first I thought maybe it was just because Elliana got sick and I was attaching some kind of emotional connection to you. But now she's better, and I find myself just..."

Daisy looked at him, unable to break his gaze. "Just what?"

"Wanting to spend all my time with you."

She felt like she couldn't breathe. How did this guy go from being the world's biggest jerk to being the most romantic man she'd ever met?

"Tristan, I think we both know this can't work. I mean, we are at two totally different levels of society. I'm a working class type of woman. You're a pent-house or mansion or private jet type of guy. And I'm your daughter's temporary nanny."

"You don't think I've been telling myself all of those things? But here's the thing... I don't care. I don't care about any of that. I don't even know what to call this. I just know that right now, I want to get to know you better. I want to know your favorite food and your favorite color and your most embarrassing moment. I just want to know *you*."

She thought for a moment about how he really didn't know her at all. He thought he did, but he definitely didn't. Maybe this would be an opportunity to make amends by telling him some truthful facts about herself.

"Pizza, blue and my most embarrassing moment is when I walked through the cafeteria in middle school and slipped on something wet and fell underneath the table while holding my tray full of food."

He laughed loudly. "That's terrible! What happened?"

"Well, I managed not to spill my food in the process, but everybody was looking at me and laughing. So, I just stayed under there."

"You stayed under the table?"

"Yep. The entire lunch. I ate my food and waited for everyone to leave before I got up. I was late to my next class, but there was no way I was facing those people."

He had a sad look on his face. "I'm so sorry that happened to you. If I'd have been there, I would've walked over, helped you up and invited you to sit at my table."

She smiled. "I'm not sure I believe you, but thanks for saying that."

"I like pizza too. And my favorite color is green, just in case you were wondering."

"Of course it is. Money is green."

His face fell a bit. "Do you think that's what I'm about? Money?"

"No. I'm sorry. I really don't think that about you. I guess I'm just a little intimidated by your title of billionaire."

"Well don't be. I know a lot of rich people, and I've known a lot of poor people in my life. Money has nothing to do with the kind of person someone is."

"So tell me about your most embarrassing moment."

"I don't know if you want to hear this."

"Yes, I do. I shared mine with you, so it's your turn."

"Fine. I was a little chubby when I was in middle school. I was also bullied relentlessly by this kid named Eddie. Anyway, one day on the school bus, Eddie and some of his buddies wrestled me to the ground in the back of the bus and pulled my jeans off."

"What? That's terrible! What did the bus driver do?"

"Back in those days, the bus driver really didn't do anything. I think they considered it a rite of passage to be bullied. Anyway, they threw my jeans up towards the middle of the bus and they started passing them around like a game of keep away. Finally, Eddie instructed one of his goons to throw them out the window. I watched them fly out and land on the train tracks below the bridge that we were crossing over. My family didn't have much money, and those were my only good jeans."

"I'm so sorry. That's terrible. Bullies stink!"

"I survived. But getting off the bus in front of everybody with my little plaid boxer shorts and having to walk all the way home was not exactly a good time."

"What ever happened to Eddie?"

"Believe it or not, he's an accountant. Calls

himself Edward now. I let him do my taxes one time when I first started my business."

"You're kidding! Why would you ever have trusted him?"

"Because I think everybody has the ability to change. No matter what terrible thing you do, you always have the option to turn it around and be forgiven. We all make mistakes. Plus, I'd like to see him try to steal my jeans now," he said, laughing.

Daisy sat there for a moment, unable to speak. If she told him the truth right now, would he forgive her? Would they still have a chance at possibly making a relationship? But she decided she was still too scared to chance it. This moment was so perfect, and this man was so amazing that she just couldn't risk it.

"I think you're awesome," Daisy said.

"Ditto."

"I guess we should be getting back?"

"Probably so. And look, I'm already dry enough to put my shirt back on." She watched him as he stood up and slid his T-shirt back over his toned, muscular chest. She couldn't help but look. She wasn't a nun, after all.

"I also meant to tell you that I'm sorry about your mall project. I know that was a blow to you."

"Yeah, I still don't understand how that happened. But I'm just going to take it as a sign. I'm kind of glad it happened, honestly."

"Really? Why?"

"Because I needed to spend more time with my daughter anyway, and the project was going to take me out of town a lot. So I'm going to use that time to strengthen my relationship with Elliana. In fact, I'm going to make a lot of changes when I get back home. My priorities have been out of whack for a long time, and this trip has taught me what's really important."

Daisy smiled as they walked back toward the hospital. He was no longer holding her hand because there wasn't a need, but she felt a huge void that she hadn't expected.

CHAPTER 13

Elliana had been so happy to leave the hospital that she literally did a little dance when they got out onto the sidewalk. Little did she know how stressful it had been on both Tristan and Daisy for those couple of days.

The next several days were a whirlwind as they got Elliana settled into the beach house and continued to nurse her back to health. The first couple of days were a little dicey, and they thought they might have to go back to the hospital once, but then she took a turn and started to get better rapidly.

Tristan had cut back on his work so much that Daisy was amazed. She watched him go from being such a staunch businessman to a doting father only concerned about his daughter's health.

They spent a lot of time together like a family, and Daisy was starting to get used to the idea that something might actually happen between them.

Every time, she had to snap herself back to reality when she thought about what she had done.

"Hello?" she said, answering her phone.

"Hey! How is Elliana?" Megan asked from the other end of the line.

"She's back to her normal, peppy self. We're going down to the beach in a little bit to have a picnic."

"And Tristan Spencer?"

"He's going with us. In fact, I can't remember the last time I saw him working. He's totally changed since this happened to his daughter. And, get this, he told me he's actually glad the mall project fell apart because it gives him more time with Elliana."

"You got lucky on that one."

"Yeah, right? So, what's up?"

"I wanted to let you know that the investors from the conservation group have been asking about your property."

"Really? Why would they want my property?"

"Apparently they're interested in using it as their office since it abuts that property they purchased."

"Interesting."

"Wait a minute... You're not actually thinking about selling your grandparents' place are you?"

"I mean, it wasn't something I was looking to do, but I wouldn't totally rule it out."

Megan sat quietly on the other end of the phone for a moment. "I don't understand, Daisy. You went through all of this to protect the property, and now you're willing to let it go?"

"A lot has changed. I guess I'm more open to the possibilities that life might have to offer me. And I've been thinking..."

"About what?"

"About staying in January Cove. In fact, I talked to the lady who owns the local coffee shop this morning and she's going to be renting out the apartment above it. She's also looking for an assistant manager, so I was thinking..."

"You're moving there? Permanently?"

"I'm just thinking about it. I like it here. And when Tristan and Elliana leave to go back home, I have to start some kind of life. I feel like I need a clean slate."

"You can't leave me. What am I going to do without you?"

Daisy laughed. "You can always come with me. I'm looking for a roommate."

"Don't tempt me. You know how much I love the beach!"

"So would you like to put in your application to be my roommate then?"

"Application? Out of the two of us, I should be more concerned about your history than mine."

For the next few minutes, Daisy recounted everything that had happened in the last several days. The time that she and Tristan had walked on the beach, the things he'd said...

"So he admitted he has feelings for you?"

"Seems that way."

"Do you have feelings for him?"

"I think I do. But I can't. There's no way I'm starting a relationship on a mountain of lies."

"I'm sorry that you're in this situation, Daisy. I wish I had some advice to help you untangle this mess."

Daisy sighed. "I was never good at word problems, and this feels like one giant, unsolvable word problem."

After hanging up with Megan, Daisy walked downstairs. Elliana was out playing in the sand, enjoying the first day she'd been totally well. Tristan was standing on the deck waving at her and laughing.

"It's so good to see her out there having fun again," Daisy said as she walked up beside him.

"It is. She gave me quite a scare. Where were you?"

"Oh, I was just chatting on the phone with my best friend. Telling her about my possible future plans."

"Future plans?"

"Well, I think I might be staying in January Cove. I have a job lined up and an apartment."

"What? Are you serious?"

"Yeah. I just feel like I need to take the next step in life. I can't stay in my small town forever, and I like the people here. I just want something brand new. So I'm going to be working at Jolt, the coffee shop down the street. And there's a little apartment above it that I'm going to be renting. And my best friend might actually join me as my roommate!"

Tristan smiled, but it was forced. He didn't look like he was exactly happy for her.

"What's the matter?"

"I don't know. I guess I was just thinking about all of this ending and me and Elliana going home. I like it here too. In some ways, I might be a little jealous that you get to stay here."

Daisy bumped his shoulder with hers. "You realize that you're a billionaire, right? You could buy the entire town if you wanted to. What's stopping you from moving here?"

"Oh, just that billion dollar business I run. And Elliana's school and friends..."

"All minor details. I assure you, that little girl down there would be happy as a clam – pun intended – to live at the beach. And she made some great friends at the dance studio who live here full-time. She keeps telling me about some little girl named Haley."

"I'm sure you're right. It's more about my business. I just can't imagine running it from here when all of my contacts are in Atlanta and other big cities."

"Tristan, you can run a business from anywhere. That's what a cell phone and a computer are for. Maybe something else is keeping you from making such a big move."

"Like what?"

"I don't know. I guess you have to figure that out for yourself."

She knew in her mind that it was probably his hesitation about living near her and making a firm commitment. She wasn't about to say anything because who was she to judge?

Daisy was becoming all too accustomed to living as a small family with Tristan and Elliana. She was worried about how she was going to react when they were gone from her life for good. It had been such a long time since she felt like she was part of a family that she really didn't want to let that go. And she loved Elliana, almost in a motherly way. She hadn't expected that at all.

She walked downstairs after tucking her in and reading her a story. Although she was doing a lot better, she still had moments of fatigue, especially after playing out in the sun. So when she was asleep, she was dead to the world until morning. She found Tristan standing at the bottom of the stairs, a smile on his face. All of the lights were out except for a couple of candles on the small table outside on the deck.

"What's going on?"

He reached out his hand and took hers as she stepped off the last step. "Come with me."

"Okay..." she said as she followed him out the French doors onto the deck.

She looked at the table and saw two dinner plates, each with a silver lid on it like at some fancy hotel. There were also two glasses of wine and an open bottle in the middle. Soft jazz music was playing from Tristan's phone which sat on one of the glass tables next to the lounge chairs.

"I didn't get a chance to ask you before, but would you go on a date with me sometime?"

She smiled. "Yes, I would. But what would you have said if I said no?" she asked, looking around at the scene.

"I would've cried," he said with a straight face. Daisy laughed.

"How did you do all of this?"

"That whole billionaire thing. I called up a local restaurant and had them whip up a little date night feast for us. There's an amazing cheesecake in the refrigerator right now."

"This is unbelievable. No one has ever done anything like this for me before."

"Well, I knew we wouldn't get to go out to a

restaurant anytime soon, so I brought the restaurant to us."

"And the music?"

"A little after dinner dancing."

He walked over and pulled out her chair. Daisy sat down, her hands shaking in her lap.

Tristan sat down across from her, a satisfied smile on his face. "I hope you like Chicken Cordon Bleu?"

"If I had any idea what that was, I could answer your question. But I like chicken, so I feel safe saying I like whatever that was you just said."

Tristan chuckled. "It's French. And it's good."

"I trust you."

"That's good because I trust you too, Daisy. More than anyone I've ever known."

Sadly, she wanted to get up and run from the table. Never had she felt so guilty in her entire life. She hadn't expected to fall for this guy. She had expected to hate him and have no problem derailing his business plans for her town. Now, here she sat, head over heels for this guy and moving away from the town she had wanted to save.

"Did I say something wrong?" he asked.

"No. Not at all."

He uncovered their plates, and Daisy hadn't seen food that fancy in her entire life. But it looked like the most succulent thing she'd ever seen. They ate and laughed and told stories from their childhoods.

She was surprised to learn that Tristan really hadn't come from money. His family had struggled, but he had done well in school and gotten scholarships which ultimately led him to making contacts to build his business. He had worked so hard for so long, and she had so much respect for him.

She talked about her grandparents and how much she loved them and losing her own mother at such a young age. She almost mentioned Thornhill a couple of times and had to stop herself. The worst part was she couldn't remember the fake town she'd made up so she kept skipping over saying the name.

They talked about Elliana and how great she was and his hopes and dreams for her future.

It was the easiest, most relaxed date she'd ever had. And he was a freaking billionaire. But he was the most down-to-earth person she'd ever sat across the table from. How had she so misjudged him at the beginning?

"Ready for dessert?" he asked.

Daisy leaned back and breathed in deep.

"Not yet. I don't think I have anywhere to put it."

Tristan stood up and reached out his hand. "Dance with me."

"Okay, but I think I should warn you that I'm not the world's best dancer."

"That makes two of us." She stood up and they walked a few feet away from the table. She slid her arms around his neck as he pulled her close, his hands firmly around her waist. She couldn't help but stare up into his crystal clear blue eyes and wonder how someone hadn't snatched him up yet.

"Thank you for such a wonderful evening."

"You deserve the world, Daisy. I hope you know that."

"Tristan, I..."

She didn't know what she was about to say. She wanted to say so many things, like how he didn't know her at all or how she had feelings for him but had lied to him. She wanted to confess everything, but she was too much of a chicken to do it.

"Don't say anything. I know all of this is really up in the air. I know you're unsure of what to do or how this would ever work. But for tonight, can we just be two people on a first date that is going very, very well?"

Daisy smiled up at him. "Okay. We can absolutely do that."

They swayed to the music for what seemed like hours, but was really only a few minutes. She found herself getting closer and closer to him. Her arms slipped off of his neck and instead went around his waist, her cheek pressed to his chest. She could feel his heartbeat, going almost as fast as hers.

And then it happened. He wasn't asleep this time when he took one hand and slid it up the side of her neck, cradling the back of her head. She looked up at him, and in a moment, his lips were pressed hers.

They were warm and inviting, and she could've gotten lost in them forever.

They stood there, kissing over and over like they couldn't stop. Like both of them were dehydrated from months in the desert and just found a well of unlimited water. She never wanted this moment to end. She never wanted him to leave January Cove or even her side. She was in too deep and getting deeper by the minute.

When they finally came up for air, they stood there, foreheads pressed together. "I have something to tell you," Daisy said.

"Okay. Please tell me it's not bad news or that will totally ruin the moment," he said, letting out a breathless laugh.

"That wasn't our first kiss."

"What?" he said, pulling back and looking at her.

"The kiss you had the dream about... It was real. You kissed me in your sleep."

Tristan's mouth dropped open. "Really? Why didn't you tell me?"

"I didn't want to make a big thing out of it because I didn't know if it meant anything."

"It meant everything, Daisy. I can't believe you lied to me," he said poking her in the side.

"Sorry."

"Okay, I forgive you... As long as that's the only lie you tell me," he said as he pulled her in and hugged her.

Yes, Tristan. That's the only lie. Ugh.

After their date, things just got more and more intense. Tristan and Daisy started spending a lot more time together, holding hands, watching movies at night after Elliana went to bed. She could feel herself getting closer and closer to him, yet she knew it was wrong. He was leaving soon. They only had a couple of weeks of summer left. She needed to break this off, but she just couldn't. She loved him, although neither one of them had said it yet.

"Where are you going ?" he asked as he walked up behind her in the kitchen and slid his arms around her waist.

"Well, if I don't go to the grocery store, we're all going to go hungry," Daisy said, enjoying the feel of his lips nestling her neck.

"I can go with you."

"No. Remember you promised Elliana that you'd fly a kite with her, and she's already out there waiting."

She pointed at Elliana who was sitting on the deck, kite in her lap, staring at her father through the window.

"She's giving me the evil eye, so I guess I better go. But I'll miss you while you're gone," he said, sneaking a kiss on her cheek. So far, they had tried to keep their relationship a secret from Elliana, but she had caught them a couple of times twirling around in the kitchen or holding hands. She wasn't stupid, so Daisy was pretty sure she knew what was going on.

"I'll be home soon," she caught herself saying. Home. As if they were a real couple with a real home. She knew all of this was about to end, and it couldn't go any further. Somehow, after he left, she'd have to cut off communication and try to get her self respect back after doing such a stupid thing.

In the end, she had ruined the opportunity to be with a man she loved because of her own deceit. And then she'd been so cowardly as to not even tell the truth. But for some reason, that felt like protecting him. Like if she never told him, he would only have good memories of her until she cut off communication and disappeared from his life.

And hurt Elliana. She knew it would hurt Elliana. And she had no idea how to avoid that.

Tristan went outside with his daughter and taught her how to fly a kite. They had a wonderful time running up and down their little stretch of beach, pulling the butterfly shaped kite high above them. The ocean winds were whipping up fiercely, so eventually they had to stop before one of them ended up going airborne.

They sat down on the beach together and stared out over the water.

"Have you had a good summer?"

"Yeah! Except for the hospital."

"Yes, that wasn't exactly a fun time for any of us," Tristan said.

"Do you love Daisy?"

Her question startled him. What was he supposed to say? He sat for a moment, quietly reflecting.

"I like her a lot," he said. He did love her, but he wasn't going to tell his daughter that before he told Daisy. He was waiting for just the perfect moment to say it.

"Are you going to marry her?"

"I don't know, sweetie. That's a long way off."

"I hope you do. I love her."

Hearing his daughter say that about Daisy made his heart swell. She felt like the perfect fit for their family, like a puzzle piece he'd never realized was missing. In truth, the future he saw always had Daisy in it. He wanted her to be his wife one day, but he also knew that he couldn't rush things for his own heart and Elliana's.

"She loves you too."

"But why did she delete your text?" Elliana asked.

Tristan froze in place.

"What are you talking about, honey?"

"In the hospital. When that man sent you a text. I heard her tell her friend that you got a text and she was going to delete it. Something about going to the mall?"

Tristan's heart started racing. He could feel the emotions welling up inside of him. Confusion. Anger. Betrayal. Surely, Eliana had just imagined that. Daisy would never do such a thing. What reason would she have?

"You must be mistaken, Elliana. Daisy would never do that."

"I was awake. I heard her talking on the phone and saying that she needed to delete your text. And then she said something about going to the mall."

He knew his daughter wasn't lying. There was no way she could've known about that missing text.

"Elliana, sit here for a minute. I need to make a quick phone call."

He walked up to the deck and pulled out his phone, dialing a long time friend back in Atlanta. "Hey Bill? I need you to do me a favor."

Bill had been a private investigator for over thirty years, so Tristan knew he would get to the bottom of this. The only problem was, he wasn't sure he wanted to know the real truth.

When Daisy got home from the grocery store, she felt a difference in Tristan's attitude.

She couldn't put her finger on it, but it was like he was angry with her.

Elliana was nowhere to be seen. "Where's El?"

Tristan didn't turn around. He stood on the deck, staring out at the ocean. "I called her new little friend, Haley's, mom. They came and took her with them to get ice cream and ride some rides at the fair."

"Oh. That means we have a little time alone. Maybe we can take a walk on the beach or..."

"You're not a nanny."

"What?"

"I said you're not a nanny," Tristan turned around, an angry look in his eyes. He stared at her with such an intensity that it made her uncomfortable.

"I don't know what you..."

"Why did you do this? Are you some kind of con artist?"

"What?"

"I know that you aren't the nanny I hired. Is your angle to get money or what?" His voice was hateful and cutting. She couldn't believe this was the same man she had left before she went grocery shopping.

"No, of course not. I've never asked you for money..."

"Then why? Why did you show up here and pretend to be the nanny?"

She realized he knew everything. He probably

knew more than everything. Her heart sank, and she felt like throwing up. The one thing she had hoped would never happen was happening right now, and she had no idea what to say or do.

"Tristan, I wasn't pretending about how I feel about you or Elliana..."

"I could have you arrested, you know. For impersonating someone and damaging my business."

She stood there, hanging her head, trying to figure out the right words to say. But there were no right words for what she had done.

"Please let me explain."

"I fell in love with you. I was going to tell you in some big romantic gesture, but I don't even know who you are."

"I fell in love with you too. I didn't expect to love you and Elliana so much. I was just trying to right a wrong, and I realized too late what I was doing..."

"You conned me. I trusted you. Elliana trusted you. She loves you. She told me so today. She wanted you to marry me so we could be a family. And the whole time you were lying to us! She's going to be heartbroken!"

He turned back around, gripping the deck with his hands as he stared out over the ocean.

"I'm from Thornhill. I was a part of that environmental group. I came here to confront you about your involvement, and when you answered the door and thought I was the nanny, I went with it. I thought I could change your mind or derail your deal."

He laughed under his breath and then turned around. "Well you certainly derailed it, didn't you? If I thought I could get any money out of you, I'd sue you until you were living under a bridge."

His words hurt. He hated her, and he was not afraid to show it.

"I'm so sorry. I never intended to hurt you or Elliana. I just didn't know how to get out of this mess. I was so scared I'd lose what we were building..."

"But you deleted the text at the hospital. You could've just not done that. You could have just left it alone, but you deleted it. That was only a couple of weeks ago."

"I know. It was a split second decision. I thought I wanted to save my town from a giant shopping mall. In the end, I realized that you and Elliana are my home."

"Get out. Get your things and get out before my daughter gets back."

"I can't say goodbye? Don't you think that's going to upset her?"

"Don't worry about my daughter," he said stepping forward and pointing his finger. "I will take care of her like I always have. I should've known I couldn't trust you. I've never been able to trust any woman. Now, get your things and get out."

Without another word, Daisy walked inside and up the stairs to pack her things. She had never expected it to end like this, but she knew she deserved it. Her short lived romance with Tristan Spencer would only be a memory, something she would tell her grandchildren one day if she wasn't too embarrassed to tell the story.

CHAPTER 14

*S*ix Weeks Later

Daisy turned the lock of the coffee shop and flipped the sign from open to closed. It had been a whirlwind few weeks after leaving Tristan and Elliana so abruptly. Megan had driven down with her things and Daisy's. Thankfully, Rebecca, who owned Jolt, had allowed them to move into the apartment above the coffee shop quickly.

She and Megan had gotten it decorated, a beach theme, of course, and Megan had started a job working at the bookstore. For the most part, they loved life in January Cove, but Daisy couldn't help but think about Tristan every day. And Elliana. She missed the little girl so much that her eyes welled with tears every time she thought about her.

They'd left four weeks ago. She hadn't heard from Tristan, not even a text. The letter she had left in her bedroom that day had apparently not done anything to change his mind or his heart about her. How could she expect that? What she had done was beyond forgiveness.

She wiped down the counters and stared out into the street, watching tourists and townspeople pass by. Everyone seemed so happy, laughing and holding hands and licking ice cream cones. Inside, she was as unhappy as she had ever been.

The sale of her grandparents' place would be final soon. She hadn't even gone back to say goodbye. Something about seeing that land after she had tried so hard to save it was just too hard for her to do. She wanted to remember it fondly before she had become such a deceitful person trying to save it.

Once she got that money, she would be able to start saving up for her own house. Maybe she and Megan would buy something on Main Street and really put down roots in January Cove. At least she'd always have her memories of Tristan and Elliana there.

It was good to have her best friend living with her. She wanted to at least have somebody around who knew her and loved her and understood she wasn't a bad person at heart.

She thought about Tristan all the time. Had he been dating already? Was he going to press charges against her?

But mostly she thought about the look on his face when he found out who she was. Or who she wasn't.

She turned around to start cleaning the cappuccino machine when she heard a knock at the door.

"We're closed..." she said to herself. It was Sunday, and they closed at 6 o'clock on the dot. All she wanted to do was go upstairs, bury her face in a bag of potato chips and watch something mindless on Netflix.

She heard a knock at the door again. "Good Lord, some people can't take a hint."

She turned around and was shocked to see Tristan standing on the other side of the glass. He was alone, wearing a pair of white golf shorts and a gray T-shirt. He looked beautiful, like some sort of mirage out in the desert.

She slowly walked towards the door, worried that he had a restraining order or a subpoena in his hand. That didn't make sense, but she was worried just the same.

She unlocked the door, and she stood there silently staring at him. He was so close. She could reach out and touch him. She wanted to, but she knew that would be the wrong thing to do.

"Hi," he said. "Can I come in?"

"Of course."

He followed her inside, and she locked the door

behind him. They walked over to one of the tables and sat down.

"I guess you're wondering why I'm here?"

"Sort of."

"I'm kind of wondering that myself."

"I thought you left."

"I did.

"Is Elliana okay?"

"She's doing very well. She misses you. She's back home with our new nanny. Actually, I moved one of my employees over to the nanny position, so Elliana has known her for years. They get along well."

"Oh. That's good. I miss her so much."

"One of the reasons I came here was to give you your final paycheck. I didn't exactly get a chance to give it to you... before you left."

He pulled an envelope out of his pocket and slid it across the table. "Thank you. I appreciate you bringing it here."

Tristan stared at her for a long moment. "I miss you."

"You do?"

"I mean, I miss the person I thought you were. I don't know what to do with those feelings."

Daisy sighed. "You do know the real me, Tristan. That wasn't a fake. I didn't tell you who I really was at the beginning, and yes I did delete that text message, but everything else was real. Every story I told you, every feeling I had. I made a huge mistake and then I made it worse on a daily basis. I should've told you. I was just too scared to lose what we were building."

"I read your letter."

"And?"

"I want you to know that I've never felt for anyone what I felt for you."

"Felt? As in past tense?"

He paused. "No. I still feel that way. I just don't know if I can trust you."

"I understand. Thank you for bringing the check. Please tell Elliana that I love her."

Daisy stood up and started walking back to the counter. Tristan stood up as well.

"Where are you going?"

"What is there to say, Tristan? I screwed up. Big time! But you don't trust me, and I can't make you trust me. What do you want from me?"

"I want you to fight! I want you to say that you can't live without me and that you love me! Like one of those chick flicks!"

Daisy couldn't help but laugh. "That's what you want? For me to make some grand romantic gesture?"

Tristan shrugged his shoulders. "I don't know. I don't know how this works! I've never done this before. I don't know how to make any of this better."

Daisy walked toward him, reaching down to hold one of his hands. "I love you. I never wanted to be away from you. I wasn't lying about my feelings, and I will never lie to you again. If you have a big zit on the end of your nose, I'll tell you. If you need more deodorant, I promise I'll pass that info along to you. No more lies, just complete honesty. But you have to make the decision on whether you're willing to risk being with me."

Tristan took her other hand and pulled her closer. "I'm willing to risk putting my heart in your hands again. I love you, and I can't let you go. I just can't. I just wanted to see if you felt the same."

"I do. But you live in Atlanta, and I live here now. How are we supposed to work that out?"

"That's the other reason I came here. I just signed the papers on the house we rented. It's mine now. I've decided that Elliana and I are moving here permanently. I have employees at my Atlanta office who will be doing most of the work. I'll drive in once or twice a month if I need to, but January Cove is my home now. You're here, and that means I have to be here too."

Daisy smiled. "And what were you going to do if I said I didn't want to be together?"

"Cry."

He pulled her into a tight embrace and pressed his lips against hers. Daisy couldn't imagine a more perfect ending to her day. Or a more perfect beginning to her life.

Want to read more Rachel Hanna books? Visit her website at www. RachelHannaAuthor.com!